TRAPP'S PEACE

BRIAN CALLISON was born in Manchester in 1934. He was educated at the High School of Dundee before entering the merchant navy in 1950 as midshipman with the Blue Funnel Line, sailing mainly on cargo liners to the Far East and Australia. On leaving the sea he studied at Dundee College of Art. He has held several administrative posts, including managing directorship of a construction company and general manager of a large entertainment centre.

He also served several years in the territorial army with the 51st Highland Division Provost Company, Royal Military Police, and now maintains an active connection with the sea as Head of Unit, Royal Naval Auxiliary Service.

His first phenomenally successful novel *A Flock of Ships* was published in 1970 and has been translated into many foreign languages. This was followed by *A Plague of Sailors*, *The Dawn Attack*, *A Web of Salvage*, *Trapp's War*, *A Ship is Dying*, *A Frenzy of Merchantmen* and *The Judas Ship*. No less an authority than Alistair MacLean has said, 'there can be no better adventure writer in the country today'.

Available in Fontana by the same author

A Flock of Ships
A Plague of Sailors
The Dawn Attack
A Web of Salvage
Trapp's War
A Ship is Dying
A Frenzy of Merchantmen
The Judas Ship

BRIAN CALLISON

Trapp's Peace

FONTANA/Collins

First published in 1979 by William Collins Sons & Co Ltd
First issued in Fontana Books 1980

Made and printed in Great Britain by
William Collins Sons & Co Ltd, Glasgow

CHAPTER ONE

Having your throat slit – actually laid wide open from ear to ear – isn't the sort of thing a chap could anticipate might happen to him in the middle of the English Channel in the middle of the night.

Not even when he's an Asiatic gentleman; and shouldn't really be there in the first place . . .!

But come to that, huddling in the lee of an antiquated fishing boat wheelhouse wearing nothing more than your threadbare lounge suit and floral tie to protect yourself against the razor whip of a December gale; desperately clutching the little suitcase containing all your pathetic personal treasures while praying to Allah or Mahomet or Dear Jesus at the same time – on top of trying convulsively not to be seasick as well as home sick and fear sick . . . well, you'd never really expected any of *those* mini-nightmares either, had you?

Of course you wouldn't have realized, when you left home, that there just isn't any established protocol for people like yourself. Or care. Not even one grain of concern.

Not when you happen to be a prospective illegal immigrant into the United Kingdom, anyway. Merely another retching package carried on the Blackbird Run . . .

But then your previously so-helpful benefactors – those shadowy philanthropists who'd bumped into you by sheer chance after you'd found yourself hopelessly marooned in Amsterdam or Brussels or Dieppe – and had offered to try to arrange your passage fr the last leg; 'Sorry, Rafiq, pal, but it's gonna cost yer a bit more, mind? Like about a hundred times over the legal Channel ferry fare . . .'; well *they* must have carelessly omitted to mention the fear bit. And the appalling discomfort. And the casual indifference

5

to your basic needs.

They hadn't mentioned the other part either. But in all fairness that was probably because even *they* hadn't imagined that a thing as dreadful as that could happen . . . IS HAPPENING, for pity's sake! When on one particular night in the English Channel you suddenly find your hair brutally seized; your head yanked back until your throat arches like a tight-stretched brown balloon . . . your protruding eyes briefly register one last incredulous glimpse of a hollow-ground butcher's knife slashing under . . . and *in* . . . and ACROSSSSS . . .!

Well, obviously a chap would never have contemplated a thing such as *that* happening to him, would he?

Certainly not after having paid such a high fare to that nice Captain Trapp. For a place on his Blackbird Run . . .

Trapp slouched heavily on the grime-sticky ledge, squashed his already battered nose against the wheelhouse window in order to see further than the foredeck through the scratched and filthy glass, then peered ferociously at the white-crested rollers bearing down from the west.

'Ayrabs!' he muttered petulantly, ignoring with lofty contempt a thundering sea which reared higher than the prudently extinguished masthead light. 'What the hell do *Ayrabs* want to get theirselves smuggled inter Britain for, then?'

Behind him Gorbals Wullie, balancing easily on the balls of his feet in time with the rearing, plunging motion of the seventy-foot vessel, casually allowed three spokes of wheel to meet the oncoming mountain.

'Teeth?' he postulated after deep deliberation. 'They c'n get free teeth an' that off've the Nashnul Health. Yous can get everythin' free off've the British Nashnul Health; even them wigs the poofy lads wear.'

But Trapp, treating his executive officer's dissertation on the attractions offered by a welfare-oriented United Kingdom with much the same disdain afforded to large waves, merely continued to speculate on his current

6

passenger list while, at the same time, trying uneasily to decipher the tiny warning bell ringing somewhere deep down in his subconscious.

Mind you, that twinge indicating the possible presence of danger had served him well on many previous occasions; for Captain Edward Trapp was nothing if not a natural refugee from trouble . . . a born Survivor. But then, with his background he'd simply had to have something extra going for him. Anyone who'd managed to survive for as long as Trapp – despite a lifetime of mayhem, gut-wrenching adventure and sheer bloody-minded pursuit of profit at any cost – well, anyone who still managed to cling so tenaciously to this mortal coil *and* stay as black-hearted and selfish a bastard as Trapp had . . . then they'd have had to have a built-in early-warning system, too.

Just like the one which unsettled the captain right then.

'We got seven of 'em this trip,' he brooded irritably. 'There's them three Paki's what couldn't spare a kilo of fat between 'em. But they're bound to be OK – your Pakistanis, Bangle Deshis, Calcutta Hindoos are all daft as brushes; put up wi' anythin' . . . but Ayrabs? What the 'ell do four *Ayrabs* want in the Land've Hope an' Glory?'

'*Teeth*, like I telt ye!' Gorbals Wullie stressed doggedly. 'Yous c'n get a braw pair o' choppers off've the Nashnul Hea . . .'

'Shut up!' his captain snapped abruptly, head cocked to one side.

Wullie eased the wheel and shrugged huffily. 'Och, but you never could stand tae lose an argymint . . .'

'I heard somethin', stupid,' Trapp growled. 'Di'n't you hear somethin'? A sort of scream, like. From aft?'

The scrawny seaman, still aggrieved, turned his head as a token gesture, then shrugged again. 'Only yon wind oot there. Jeeze but it's blowin' hard enough tae skin the paint right off've this worm-rotten bucket . . . if you'd ever put ony paint *on* the bloody boat in the first place!' he added spitefully.

And that was what really did it. That was the trigger to a

temporary lapse which promised to puncture rather more of Trapp than his dignity and position as a shipowner.

'PAINT!' he exploded, almost at a loss for words at the enormity, the crass extravagance of the suggestion. 'Paint costs money, remember? Apart from which I'm not goin' to have 'er tarted up to look like some millionaire's fancy floatin' gin palace. Not f'r no one . . .'

'Christ but you gotter be jokin',' Wullie sniggered recklessly, eyeing the ravages of sixty years of neglect evincing themselves in the cracked glass and started planking and peeling, rotted frames which formed the command centre and navigation space of the motor fishing vessel *Last Hope*.

But Trapp was well and truly diverted now, because if there had ever been one factor which had constantly threatened his prospects for continued survival – one flaw in the captain's bloody-minded resolve to remain the world's oldest operational pirate – then it was in his Achilles' heel of greed.

In his eternal quest for a profit. By hook or by crook – though usually by the latter. That singular need which encapsulated Edward Trapp's sole motivation, creed, and all-consuming obsession in life.

Which was why, now fully launched on his favourite subject, he swung from the window, directed a pugnacious jaw towards the cretinous ferret shape of Gorbals Wullie, and snarled heavily, '*Paint* 'er, f'r cryin' out lou . . .! But then you always *wus* bloody useless in the complex fields've commerce though, wasn't you? Got about as much financial acumen as a bankrupt Delhi dung-wallah, 'aven't you . . .? In fac' the only way you ever earned an honest livin' was ter con some pie-eyed bastard up an alley an' *boot* 'is wallet outa him, wasn't it then . . .?'

Whereupon the storm surrounding them howled unnoticed. While the creaking hull of the anything-but-good ship *Last Hope* spiralled and spluttered painfully towards the English side of the English Channel with a steadily decreasing complement.

And Trapp completely ignored that warning bell which somehow involved Arabs, never even hearing the next bubbling half-scream from six feet away on the other side of the bulkhead as a third abruptly disillusioned voyager from Pakistan felt his windpipe being severed with one expert stroke.

Which wasn't at all what he'd expected.

Not on Captain Trapp's Blackbird Run.

Perhaps that had always been Trapp's failing – apart from his basic avarice, anyway. That somehow his bloody-minded prejudice against doing the legal thing had invariably thwarted the fulfilment of every project he'd ever devised.

Even from the start; many wars and many, many years before while he'd still been a starry-eyed boy wearing his first uniform as a midshipman of His Majesty's Royal Navy. He'd promised then to do his duty to fight for King and Country with all the pride a little lad could feel . . . until the enemy sank his very first ship, and left him as the sole survivor from a complement of four hundred men.

It had been then that his gift of living to fight another day had initially revealed itself . . . except that the young Edward Trapp never did get to do his duty for the King after all. For it had been the enemy who'd found the life-raft he'd shared with a small section of a dead shipmate for nineteen horrific, lonely days; whereupon they had patched up his physical wounds, were unable to do anything about the mental scars he'd suffered – and finally locked him away in a prisoner-of-war camp until that particular war ended two years later.

By then Trapp had already become a permanent casualty of battle; a hardened, embittered self-seeker who'd learned that survival in his particular barbed-wire corner of hell was based on greed and animal cunning, reinforced by the ability to do unto others twice as much aggro as they could do unto you – an' a bit sooner.

He'd grown to detest waste with a fierce and undiminishing passion. He hated war as a folly in which men died for a futile ideal, and without ever being given the opportunity to make a profit. He developed a withering contempt for his own country and a total indifference to the problems of all others.

But he'd found one belief; one priceless, earth-conquering philosophy . . . That his destiny, no matter what he did or to whom it was done, would undoubtedly be – to survive.

And so he'd embarked on a lifetime of unabashed skull-duggery in which he quickly developed the most twisted, inconsistent set of principles any international pariah could muster. For instance, the self-styled *Captain* Edward Trapp would tenderly assist a disease-ravaged Chinese beggar-woman across a bedlam Shanghai street – yet calmly watch the hand being chopped from a Sudanese thief's wrist with a deprecating, 'It's not what you done that makes you a stupid bastard, Ali Baba. It's gettin' caught that proves you always was!'

He'd fled Macao after a somewhat fraught disagreement with a local Fu Manchu, but hadn't even bothered to warn his current Chinese lady-friend about the gathering wrath of the Tongs. Her dismembered corpse, intimately conjoined with bits and pieces of a few more of Trapp's unsuspecting acquaintances, was discovered on the lawn of the British consulate the next morning . . . Yet the very same Trapp had once spent three days of parched agonies in the desert, scrambling for his life ahead of a posse of homicidally-inclined Tuaregs, after he'd kicked their sheik on a voyage to the Pit for raping a snot-nosed, ten-a-penny Arab urchin.

He had always survived. Through all those years of pimping and conning, and chasing a fast buck by sailing in decrepit, inevitably-to-be coffin ships for some poor bloody sailorman or other. Only they never went down with Trapp aboard. No. He'd always done a pierhead jump; usually as they sailed on their last voyage.

Gradually, as he became a more and more successful

drop-out, there had been the development of his business career. Only that had proved even more confusing to any casual observer, being guided by what Trapp primly described as his 'Principles'. 'A gentleman what's engaged in internashnul commerce's gotter 'ave *Principles*!'

Which he undoubtedly had. In his own inimitable, screwed-up sort of way.

For instance, there was the manner in which Trapp first became A Shipowner.

Certainly they'd offended his sense of chivalry from the very beginning, those three Egyptian speculators, by casting unwarranted aspersions regarding the possibility of his stealing the cargo should they offer him command of their gun-running vessel *Charon*. Eventually, and in the absence of a more suitable crook, they were forced to, but Trapp was so deeply wounded by their unjustifiable cynicism that he determined to fulfil his contract with impeccable correctness, delivering every last weapon and round of ammunition to the appointed rendezvous . . .

. . . and stole the *Charon* instead.

But by then she didn't have any owners anyway – not seeing Trapp had delivered them to a waiting patrol of trigger-happy Legionnaires at the same time. As he explained so self-righteously later, 'I done what they paid me for, di'n't I? An' there wasn't nothin' in the contract about the ship, was there then . . .?'

Then there was the time when Trapp, rapidly approaching the peak of his piratical success not only as master and owner of the *Charon* – probably the oldest, most appalling heap of barely-floating rust outside a breaker's yard – but also as leader of as black a band of cut-throats and thieves as ever graced the inside of the world's prisons, including, incidentally, one Gorbals Wullie frae Glasgae an' Barlinnie Jail . . . when Trapp got involved, in a purely business sense naturally, with the Spanish Civil War. When he accepted a contract to run guns and ammunition into that strike-torn country for a very handsome price.

Which, strictly according to his principles, he did;

risking being either garrotted as a capitalist warmonger by the Reds or, alternatively, bayoneted as a suspected Bolshevik by Franco's mob. But the point is that he did carry out his commitment with religious zeal.

The only snag was that, frustrated by the waste of unprofitable stowage space still left after he'd loaded his first shipment, he then went ahead and negotiated a second contract with the *other* side to do precisely the same thing for them.

The fact that all that money was paid to Trapp without altering one jot the balance of power either way just didn't seem to worry him. But like he said – 'A contract's a contract, ain't it? An' there never was no clause innit ter say my services was excloosive, *was* there . . .?'

And so came the Second World War.

Even that didn't bother Trapp at first. He simply declared a sort of unilateral neutrality for himself and his cretinous crew, and carried on smuggling and blockade-running precisely as before.

Until he was finally brought face to face with unavoidable reality. And the Royal Navy leaned on him a little, while, characteristically, he even visualized the chance of profit in *that*. Eventually Lieutenant-Commander Trapp, RNR, took Gorbals Wullie – together with the most ill-assorted crew of military misfits the world has ever shuddered at the thought of – on an unsteady, violently unconventional course to war. Because, naturally, it was a special, very different kind of war.

It had been Trapp's War.

But that's another story . . .!*

Yet strangely enough, despite all the mayhem and double-dealing in Trapp's turbulent life, he never really became a dislikeable man. A bigoted, ill-tempered, foul-mouthed intolerant crook – well . . . yes.

But not a dislikeable man.

*Collins/Fontana

While later had followed the fringe benefits offered by all the little terror wars: Korea, Borneo, Cyprus and Aden, Vietnam, Ethiopia, even Yom Kippur . . . only he never quite managed to live up to his early intentions. Oh, he was still the eternal survivor; that much had to be admitted. But somehow, after the proper war, he never quite succeeded in his quest for that Promised Land where profit was for the taking and his decks were laid with coin.

So he never did conquer the earth.

Now it was today. And all he had in the world was an argumentatively loyal henchman called Gorbals Wullie, and a tired and virtually unseaworthy old boat called, perhaps a little cynically, the *Last Hope*.

Plus an undying, fervent optimism that one day – one day very soon – he really would find that pot of gold.

Somewhere . . .

In some credulous bugger's pocket.

. . . and then the wheelhouse door slid open, allowing a shrieking, buffeting slab of gale to enter followed by the even chillier aspect of a Czechoslovakian Model 61 sub-machinegun with a blued-steel folding stock on the end of it. And one of Trapp's carelessly forgotten Arabs on the end of that.

'. . . so I'm tellin' you, yer daft Scotch egg, that paint's *not* one o' the fripperies I'm plannin' ter throw money away on . . . Jesus CHRIST!' ended a disbelieving Trapp.

Whereupon Gorbals Wullie, moving with the reflex agility of someone well practised in the art of getting out from under while the weight dropped on the next bloke, disappeared through the opposite door in a mercurial blur with only the comment, 'Och, Jeeze, but we bin HI-jacked . . .!' left hanging in the air to prove that the *Last Hope* hadn't steered all that way on auto-pilot alone.

But admittedly Wullie's loyalty did tend to flood and ebb at times – usually the latter, when the heat came on.

Trapp, meanwhile, with the automatic response born of a lifetime in hazard, began to reach for the ancient elephant gun clipped conveniently to the deckhead above him until another dark-skinned man slipped in through the open door, placed the muzzle of an ominously large and destructive Luger at the base of Trapp's spine, and said persuasively, 'Leave it, Captain . . . please.'

So Trapp froze. Instantly. But that was something else he'd learned from a lifetime of surviving – that a pistol in the hand is worth two cannons out of reach.

. . . just as Gorbals Wullie reappeared again, this time going astern very, very cautiously indeed; eyes fixed hypnotically on the butcher's knife held unwaveringly against his middle region.

And without blinking even once, muttered resentfully, 'This is anither fine mess yous has got me intae, Captin!'

'Oh, shut up!' Trapp snarled nervously, yet still mindful of his property. 'An' get back on the wheel afore she broaches-to an' dammiges somethin'.'

The man with the automatic barked in guttural Arabic and the knife withdrew a little reluctantly from Wullie. But not all that far. Then the *Last Hope* slid into a corkscrew roll while Trapp watched warily for the first sign of instability among his visitors, only there wasn't any. They were very good indeed.

So instead he spent his rising fury on the scrawny figure of his first lieutenant, currently attempting to ease past the knife-point to reach the wheel without committing involuntary hara-kiri during the next beam sea.

'Hurry UP!' he roared. 'Another like that'll cost me a mint f'r repairs . . .' Then the nightmare prospect of actually having to spend money got just too much for him and he rounded spitefully on the man behind him, ignoring the gun altogether.

'An' YOU . . .' he spluttered, virtually beside himself with rage. 'You c'n jus' get off've my ship right now, savee? You an' your oppos. 'Cause you got as much chance as a snowball in hell of me landin' you in Britain after this . . . and the contract's cancelled, see? Without no bloody refund!'

But the man facing him only smiled. It was almost a friendly smile. Almost. 'But we do not propose to go to Britain, Captain.'

Then a mocking twinkle showed in the dark eyes. 'Anyway, *effendi* – whatever makes you imagine a poor Arab could afford to live there?'

'Ahh,' Trapp said cleverly. 'I knew you wus Ayrabs. I even said you wus bloody Ayrabs the minnit I set eyes on you . . . an' Ayrabs is trouble; especially you educated ones. So which are you then – Al Fatah, Black September, them PLOs . . . ?'

'None, Captain.' The leader shrugged. 'I regret to say we seem to be simply common or garden criminals . . .'

From behind the wheel Gorbals Wullie appended a professional amendment. 'So it's no' a hi-jack, Captin – it's a heist.'

'Shut UP!' Trapp retorted with childish predictability. 'And anyway, seein' this ain't no jumbo jet – an' while she's worth a good few dollars on the open market I wouldn't exactly claim she's as valuable as the QE Two – jus' what in Saint Elmo's fire d'you want 'er for?'

'We don't,' the Arab assured him. 'It's you we want, Captain Trapp.'

'Come ter that,' Trapp continued introspectively, 'I'd've sold her to you f'r less than you paid that shifty git what fixed your Blackbird passage up in Brusse . . . *What* did you say?'

'I said it is you we want, Captain. So permit me to introduce myself. My name is . . . ah . . . Fadel. That should be quite adequate for now.'

A heavy sea shook the *Last Hope* angrily, but this time Trapp didn't even glance up at the gun as the warning bell inside him began to clang with positive hysteria. Gorbals Wullie on the other hand, hopefully relieved by the assumption that, seeing they wanted Trapp, then pre-sumably *he* wasn't personally involved, offered in-gratiatingly, 'Aye? Then it's no' a heist either. It's a kidnapping, Capt . . .'

'*Shut up!*' Trapp bellowed in escalating apprehension. 'An' whaddyou mean – it's *me* you want . . .?'

Then an even more unsettling doubt struck him and he broke off sharply, staring round. For he'd suddenly remembered he'd had seven immigrants on the after deck when they sailed; but now there were only four in the wheelhouse.

'Them Pakis,' he specified uneasily. 'They started off down aft with you. Didn't . . . they . . . then . . .?'

Which was the moment when he ground to a halt altogether as his eyes and Wullie's pivoted simultaneously to fix on the butcher's knife. Even in the dim glow from the compass it was possible to detect the sticky red film which covered it.

'Och, Jeeeeze,' Wullie whispered, the cobwebbed recesses of his mind slowly deducing that, even though he didn't actually appear to be a kidnap victim himself, he was still more than likely to be involved. In a very personal sense indeed.

Trapp swallowed. 'But why that way, mister? Guns is quicker. An' cleaner . . . and kinder, come to that.'

The man with the Luger – the one called Fadel – shrugged, holding his watch into the light from the binnacle as if time held considerable importance. 'They are also noisy. While you have a reputation for being a resourceful and violent person . . .'

He smiled fleetingly, only there wasn't any humour in it at all. '. . . and after all; you say we are only troublesome Arabs, Captain. So why criticize us for being cut-throats and . . . ah . . . traditionalists, shall we say?'

'I also got a reputation f'r carryin' out my contracts,' Trapp ground bitterly. 'I had a contract with them poor bastards to deliver 'em ashore. In good condition.'

'I cancelled it.' Fadel gestured with finality. 'No more

questions. It is time.'

Immediately the Arab with the machinegun moved forward, nestling the muzzle into Trapp's midriff. Even under the frantic motion of the *Last Hope* the barrel remained as steady as if it were gyro-stabilized.

And so did Edward Trapp.

Apart from his eyes. For after his initial disconcertion Trapp was again the total survivor; the quintessence of durability. In his characteristic way he was even strengthened by that surge of animal cunning which always peaked as his back came hard against the wall. He was ageless and matchless, and lethal as a cornered rattlesnake.

Trapp. With a burning fuse . . .

But until the opportunity presented itself he would simply watch while wrestling furiously with the riddle of why Fadel and his Arabian bully-boys should wish to abduct *him* – a hostage whom nobody would ransom, and without a country which would wish to negotiate his release. And why, in *God's* name, should they deliberately do this in such a coldly horrific way?

For he was not the sort to forget those three little brown men – his cargo and his responsibility – who'd risked everything for the new life awaiting them at the end of their particular rainbows; yet had drowned so gruesomely in their own blood instead.

Whereupon Edward Trapp grew more and more angry. And more and more dangerous . . .

He looked on impassively while the leader, Fadel, produced a small walkie-talkie and spoke briefly, commandingly, into it.

All Trapp could detect was an answering crackle of guttural Arabic which meant nothing to him at all because he, even after a lifetime as a world wanderer, had never bothered to learn more than a few coarse phrases of any foreign tongue. More pertinently, those scant VHF transmissions wouldn't convey any information to the many listeners surrounding the English Channel.

Which suited Trapp anyway. An investigation by either the French or UK authorities would merely have transferred him from a Middle Eastern frying-pan into a very long-term European fire. There were many curious immigration officers anxious to have a little chat about his Blackbird connections, and an even greater number of frustrated detectives on both sides of the Channel searching for answers to certain questions raised with monotonous regularity since around 1929. And all involving a certain Captain Edward Trapp . . .

He even maintained his grim self-control when Fadel calmly reduced the clanking engine revolutions to 'Slow' without so much as a by-your-leave to him, Trapp, master before God aboard his own ship – or boat, really; but Trapp always had been a bit inclined to gild his own lilies.

Trapp watched as the *Last Hope* mintained bare steerage way, while the great black waves swept down on them from out of the darkness with the wind clawing mournfully at the tattered, rotting strands of rigging, and sometimes a sea, larger or more deceitful than the rest, tumbled inboard over the scarred bulwarks to atomize spitefully against the decrepit wheelhoue.

All that time he assessed the faces of the men around him; studied them in minute detail. Darkly saturnine in the binnacle glow these were the emotionless, uncompromising faces of men doing a professional task, without the slightest guilt or regret for what had occurred on the after deck.

Apart from Gorbals Wullie, of course; now struggling to keep the skyrocketing bows turned into the sea. For Wullie's pinched features were shiny with the sweat of fear, and sickly white with the realization that – if it was only Trapp they hd come for – then he was quite likely to be as expendable as . . . well . . . as three little immigrants.

Before Trapp caught Wullie's eye, then glanced meaningfully up at the deckhead – and at the ancient elephant gun which the hijackers had contemptuously ignored while a look passed between them which made Wullie sweat even more because Gorbals Wullie knew better than anybody else – or anybody else alive, at least – just how big a chance Trapp was prepared to take to preserve his freedom.

And, more practically, his property.

So Trapp waited. And watched. And remembered.

Until they saw the ship . . .

CHAPTER TWO

It came into sight twenty minutes later; a distant masthead light at first, barely visible through the rain and the black overcast of the Channel night. Then, briefly between wave crests, they began to make out the red and green sidelights as it headed towards them until finally the bulk of the vessel could be detected against the gloom.

To Trapp at that time it was simply another ship on a closing course, so he watched with mounting unease until he could even glimpse the foam flinging in wide phosphorescent gouts from under the looming bow.

'Starb'd the wheel,' he snapped finally. 'We better give way or she'll be into us.'

The man, Fadel, merely said, 'Stay on course, Captain. She knows we are here. They will have us on radar and are expecting us.'

'Expectin'?' Trapp growled. Then swore explosively as the sub-machinegun barrel ground warningly into his ribs.

'I said no more questions,' the leader murmured, eyes fixed on the approaching vessel. 'Now you will please switch on your own navigation lights. Soon they will lose us in their radar clutter.'

'Bugger off!' Trapp snarled uncompromisingly.

Fadel didn't get angry or offended or anything else. He simply shrugged calmly, turned to face Gorbals Wullie, then motioned with the Luger. Immediately the two Arabs standing behind the scrag-end helmsman moved as one, pinioning his arms before he could even emit a startled yelp. One half-blink of a blind man's eye later and the undernourished figure was arched backwards across the wheel, hair entangled savagely in one practised hand while the red glint of the knife slashed horizontally inwards and towards . . .

'WAIT!' Trapp bellowed, suddenly terrified for Wullie.

The knife halted within a millisecond of death, almost touching the furiously convulsing Adam's apple. 'Mary Mother o' *God*!' Wullie choked hysterically. '*Dae* it, Captin! Put they bluidy LIGHTS ON . . .!'

Trapp closed his eyes momentarily, to stop anyone detecting the frustration in them. Because he knew he'd lost the best chance he was ever going to get of turning the tables; that one brief moment in which all attention had been focused on the long overdue – in Trapp's usually jaundiced opinion – task of cutting Gorbals Wullie's throat.

Only now he'd blown it. Because he'd suddenly found to his consternation that he wasn't quite such a self-centred and flint-hard bucko as he'd prided himself on being.

An' there weren't all that many sailormen around who'd work as cheap as Gorbals Wullie either . . .

'The lights, Captain?' Fadel suggested pointedly.

'Ohhhh shit!' Trapp snarled. Then snapped the switch.

'Flash them three times to identify ourselves. The ship will stop and you will take this boat alongside. They will make a lee for us and have a pilot ladder rigged . . . do you understand?'

'Then what?'

'Just do it! Or should I still use your friend as an incentive . . .?'

'Aw Jeeeeze,' Wullie spluttered, still transfixed across the wheel. Trapp glowered briefly at the poised knife, then sniffed.

'Let 'im go, then! How's 'e supposed to steer, all spread out like a paralytic bloody starfish?'

Fadel nodded and the two heavies abruptly released the little Glaswegian. Wullie's knees gave way and he slid to the deck before tentatively hauling himself vertical again and grasping the wheel.

Trapp eyed Wullie's usually permanently-glued-on-the-back-of-his-head cloth cap lying where it had fallen, and gestured.

'Put yer cap on again.

Wullie blinked nervously, still leaning as far away from the knife-point as stability would allow.

'Whit?'

'Yer CAP, stupid – put it back on yer 'ead!' Trapp urged meaningfully. 'I'm not 'avin' my chief officer improperly dressed now, am I? Not at the very moment we . . . go . . . along*side*, like?'

'You're awfy posh all of a sudden,' Wullie muttered blankly.

'Christ!' Trapp reflected savagely to himself, 'the only way that half-witted Scotch moron's ever gonna get the message is if I shove it up 'im wi' a ten-foot boat 'ook!'

But Wullie's vacant stare showed a glimmer of animal cunning. He looked down at the cap – then surreptitiously up at the elephant gun – and said cleverly, 'Och, jus' look at *that*, then. Ah've forgotten tae put ma bonnet on . . .'

Whereupon he bent down, crammed the cap on the back of his lank skull, and adjusted the peak with exaggerated sartorial care.

In fact with very great care indeed . . .

And so they waited for the ship to reach them.

Only, this time, neither Trap nor Gorbals Wullie seemed quite so frustrated.

Almost co-operative, somehow. And not at all dangerous.

The ship lay stopped some three cables from them, now clearly visible in silhouette and minutely scrutinized by a still-baffled Edward Trapp.

A smallish general-cargo freighter of around six thousand tons gross she was maybe ten or twelve years old. Conventional centrecastle surmounted by a squat, unimaginative funnel; single lifeboat either side and well supplemented by life-raft canisters; a high but rather ugly sheer towards the bows . . . no indication of her nationality yet, an' no bloody wonder, Trapp brooded irritably.

He decided he didn't like the anonymous vessel. Come to that, he didn't reckon he was goin' to go much on the crew she carried either.

A sudden glow bathed her forward well deck as a shaded cargo cluster was switched on. They were close enough to discern a group leaning over the starboard bulwarks, rigging a skeletal rope ladder. Fadel waited until the ladder had unrolled against the hull, then gestured imperatively with the Luger.

'It is sheltered there. You will go alongside now.'

'I *do* know which way the wind's blowin',' Trapp retorted reasonably. 'An' you might tell Chatty 'ere to put 'is gun up. I don't concentrate so good connected to a trigger-'appy sod like 'im.'

Fadel hesitated, then nodded. The sub-machinegun muzzle eased away from the captain's ribs and he exhaled gratefully. 'No tricks, either of you,' the Arab leader warned grimly. Trapp raised a shocked eyebrow.

'Who – *us*?' he protested, then turned and placed one huge, calloused hand on the throttle lever. 'Special sea dutymen close up f'r goin' alongside . . . that's you, Wullie lad!'

He eased the throttle forward and *Last Hope* came round, butting doggedly into the sea with the spray, snatched by the wind, once again hissing angrily across her decks.

'We could have had the windscreen wiper goin',' Trapp offered conversationally. 'If we 'ad a windscreen wiper.'

Closing fast, the high sides of the freighter looming overhead now; near enough to detect lighter patches of rust showing beneath the main engine discharge and freeing ports. But no ensign was visible, nor legible name on the bow, while her port of registry was well out of sight under her counter.

Closer still.

And closer . . .

A wave took the *Last Hope* through a forty-degree roll but she was steadying finally, coming under the lee of the bigger vessel.

'Slow down!' Fadel snapped abruptly, betraying his first

hint of nervousness beneath the cool professionalism.

'Sweat, you callous bastard!' Trapp grinned savagely to himself; then he hauled the throttle lever back while the *Last Hope* coasted steadily onwards and at an oblique angle to the steel wall.

'Engine stopped,' he called mockingly. 'But I gotter keep a bit've way on 'er so's she'll swing stern-to when we goes alongside an' . . .'

'No talking, I said,' Fadel almost snarled while, beside him, the mute with the sub-machinegun brought the barrel down warningly.

Trapp gave a philosophical shrug and faced forward again, watching critically as the gap between the two vessels narrowed fast while the reflected incandescence from the cargo cluster caused a million tiny wavelets to sparkle fleetingly around them . . . and showed as a well-polished gleam lining the twin barrels of that monstrous elephant gun still clipped above Trapp's head.

Thirty feet . . . twenty-five . . . twenty-two . . .

Twenty.

He turned, still casually gripping the throttle. Gorbals Wullie caught his eye and dropped a querying glance to the wheel, then jerked his head imperceptibly to port. Trapp simply smiled, but it was a fleeting, immensely evil smile.

Fifteen feet and still coasting.

The heads lining the bulwarks above them were out of sight now, masked by the wheelhouse deckhead . . . the *Last Hope* penduluming on the sullen swell with the idling splutter of her engine only faintly perceptible above the closing rumble of the freighter's machinery space.

Ten feet.

'You gotter work a boat hard,' informed Trapp doggedly. 'So's she c'n feel the action of the prop against the rudde . . .'

But then he stopped. Dead. As his eyes, casually glancing outboard through the grime-dulled starboard windows, widened in slowly dawning disbelief. Until . . .

'Di'n't I SAY you wus trouble?' he blurted in outraged fury. 'By God, but you di'n't tell me you 'ad a British frigate waitin' for us as well . . .'

And then he slammed the throttle lever hard forward, roared 'HARD A PORT *NOW* . . .!' – and lunged for the deckhead while four disconcerted and momentarily confused Arabs swivelled to starboard as one man.

The *Last Hope*, already approaching its target at a broad angle, surged crazily ahead under fully-restored engine power and, at the same time, listed hugely as the sweat-shiny Gorbals Wullie spun the wheel in an apprehension-goaded blur . . .

. . . before snatching off his bonnet with what seemed curiously misplaced formality under the circumstances. And the manner in which he did it; that appeared a little unconventional too – grabbing it from the after end of his head so's the cloth peak hung free in his grime-engrained fist while maintaining the swing; arc-ing viciously in a fluttering parabola towards the astonished face of the man holding the knife.

Five feet . . . four . . . three . . .

The sub-machinegun barrel lurching back now as the Arab mute realized there simply *wasn't* any frigate out there, or any other diversion other than in Trapp's mind . . . but Trapp's great mahogany paw also dragging the elephant gun down from its clip and snatching for the twin triggers all at the same time . . . Gorbals Wullie's voice screeching, 'Yous bastids! Yous poofy hi-jackin' BASTIDS . . .!' in a fear-pitched hysteria of desperation . . .

Bedlam! And steel. A terrifying, careering steel horizon blanking everything . . .

The *Last Hope* struck the freighter virtually ed-on with sixty-odd tons of accelerating inertia. Almost immediately her rotted, ageing frames began to telescope concertina fashion in a continuous splintering rumble while every already cracked pane of glass in the wheelhouse exploded outwards in sparkling fragments.

'CHRIST!' Trapp bellowed manically above the increasingly expensive cacophony. 'She weren't meant to do *that*, dammit . . .' Then fired as his back came against the wheelhouse ledge; the only stable body – apart from an equally prepared and grimly clinging Wullie – in a rapidly disintegrating world.

The muzzle flash from the ancient weapon was almost as destructive in itself, igniting the flaked and tinder-dry paint whorls peeling from the deckhead in a rippling, spreading pool of flame while, at the same time, the Arab holding the sub-machinegun disappeared backwards through the wheelhouse door, literally taking off from a cordite-ringed spew of blood and fragmented flesh.

'Christ!' Trapp blurted again, shaken to the core by the chain reaction of devastation his subtle ploy had triggered – while the *Last Hope* continued to condense into a cloud of dry-rot dust; the foremast collapsing across the rearing, splintering bows; the galloping flamelets flickering and flashing delightedly as the coachroof itself began to burn.

And then Wullie's swinging bonnet ever so lightly stroked the cheek of the dumbfounded Arab with the knife – before miraculously opening a hideous gash from his right eye to the tip of his jaw.

But Gorbals Wullie always had been a master craftsman – indeed a positive maestro – in the braw Glasgae traditions of hand-tae-hand combat born of many deliriously happy hours as an apprentice yobbo in pub brawls, fitba' riots an' punch-ups doon at the Mocambo Ballroom.

Which was also why Gorbals Wullie never went anywhere, not even to bed, without his beloved bonnet. And the line of skilfully concealed razor blades which just happened to be sewn into the peak . . .

Pirouetting like a ballet dancer the reassured Scotsman swung to face his second guard; vengefully this time, swaying on half-crouched legs with the cap dangling warily like the sling of a ferrety David facing his Goliath.

'Fancy yer chances, dae ye, Abdul?' he grinned, yellow teeth bared in the mandatory hard-man snarl. 'C'mon then, ye big poofter, 'cause ah'm goin' tae cut ye wide open an' sti . . .!'

So Abdul *did* come on. And kicked him so hard between the half-parted legs that Wullie didn't even have the breath to scream in agony. But it had never really occurred to Gorbals Wullie that maybe they had a Mocambo Ballroom in the Casbah too . . .

. . . while Trapp started to yell a warning as both of Wullie's tormentors, one still gripping that gruesomely dappled knife while spraying blood from his mutilated features, closed in on the convulsed seaman until he – Trapp – sensed rather than saw the danger at his own feet and swung back to catch the rising glint of a Luger coming to meet him.

One stark image lit by the dancing flames of the man called Fadel, still on his knees where the impact had captured him; and the murderous glare in eyes which, until then, had merely showed a cynical contempt . . .

. . . and the nine-millimetre hole in the barrel which was nearly on him f'r . . .

Trapp snatched the second trigger in reflex, unthinking panic.

The monstrous cannon roared again. It pulverized Fadel's right arm and shoulder while igniting clothing, dust, age-old scraps of gum wrappings and discarded junk, and most of the starboard corner of the wheelhouse itself.

But the biggest snag was that, since Trapp had been unwittingly aiming downwards at the time, the cannon-ball-sized charge also blew a jagged two-foot cavity through the deck, kept right on travelling into the accommodation space abruptly revealed below, shredded Trapp's only shore-going suit and a well-thumbed copy of *How To Make A Million Overnight* . . .

. . . and finally blasted a second hole clean through the *Last Hope*'s already long-suffering hull.

Which, in its turn, immediately caused the English Channel to enter – searching in frothing, gurgling excitement for the rest of that same English Channel currently flooding aft from the shattered bow compartments.

Whereupon Trapp, by now appalled at the devastation his intended minor diversion had caused, choked a third faintly bemused 'Christ!'; then slammed the Mocambo-trained Arab vindictively across the back of his skull with the butt of the elephant gun.

Wullie, meanwhile, lying all drawn up and retching on his back on the deck, had opened his eyes eventually to observe his final assailant – pain-crazed and unmistakably homicidal – half-way through a knife-waving dive on top of him.

Wullie, terrified out of what little wits he had, simply screwed his eyes tight shut again; screeched, 'Aw, dinnae . . .! Aw, Captin, HELP me . . .!'; and kicked out convulsively in a jerky, unco-ordinated bicycling action during which one boot sole caught the flying knife-man square in the pit of his stomach . . . caused him to describe an immaculate parabola with Wullie's leg acting as a fulcrum . . . and then disappear clean through the gaping starboard window-frame on the end of a long, fading wail of disillusionment.

And, all of a sudden, everything seemed so quiet, and so very peaceful again.

Except for the frantic clamour of the *Last Hope*'s engine, still driving her against the steel side of the mystery freighter with bulldog tenacity. And the splintering sounds of still more rotten timbers compressing and crumbling. And the disconcerting crackle of little flames as they took an ever-firmer hold of Trapp's command.

'Five hundred,' Trapp muttered numbly. 'Five 'undred quid this queen o' the seas cost me. Five . . . 'undred . . . *quid*!'

Wullie rolled over and clawed to his knees, hanging on to the deserted wheel. 'See him?' he stammered with gleeful pride. 'Did ye no' see me sort him oot, then? Bang, bang! The karate chop, eh?'

Absently Trapp pulled the throttle back to neutral. Fuel

cost money. The *Last Hope* stopped trying to wear a hole in the freighter and just sat sinking instead.

'Ah'm a . . . a tiger,' Gorbals Wullie announced modestly, almost reverently. 'Ah'm no' feared o' nuthin', and that's a fact.'

'Five hundred bloody quid,' Trapp whispered; fast slipping into shock as the full financial horror of the night dawned upon him.

'Here,' the tiger said, suddenly nervous again. 'Should we no' be makin' oor getaway?'

Trapp looked around him at the carnage and the flames; and at the splintered foredeck already nearly awash. Then he turned and glared at his first lieutenant with an expression which would have withered a great white shark, far less a tiger, and snarled, 'Don't be so *bloody* silly.'

Before sticking his head through the eviscerated forward window and craning his neck upwards to meet a silent, awestruck row of dark faces lining the rails above.

'Kidnappin',' Trapp bellowed dangerously, ignoring with supreme contempt the battery of machineguns, rifles and various other small arms pointing down at him. 'Throat cuttin' . . . Arson, hi-jack, murder . . . breach o' CONTRACT . . .'

Furiously he beat at his sleeve which began to smoulder just as water came in through the wheelhouse door. 'I dunno why; an' I dunno who wants me so bad but . . .'

He hesitated briefly as a thought struck him. A typically Trapp thought.

'. . . but ONE o' you bastards up there owes me a thousand quid. F'r replacement. At nett cost.'

CHAPTER THREE

'Fifteen hundred,' Trapp muttered doggedly a few minutes later. 'Fifteen hundred quid them boys o' yours has cost me, mister . . .'

Then his voice trailed off and he found himself suffering a chill even worse than he had felt when the submachinegun had first eased ominously through his wheelhouse door.

Yet that was strange, really. Because the man facing him across the cabin of that still-anonymous freighter seemed at first sight to be a most good-humoured sort of chap; especially in view of the somewhat churlish reception Trapp had given to his emissaries a short while before.

Perhaps it was the extended and welcoming hand of the man which triggered the alarm bell in Trapp's subconscious once again; the way the beautifully manicured nails gleamed so pinkly under the lights. Or maybe the almost imperceptible trace of perfume was causing it, hanging like a sick-sweet mockery of the earlier stench of fear and violence which went down with the *Last Hope*.

And then Trapp suddenly did understand what was so unsettling about the suave, quite charming Middle Eastern gentleman before him – it was the expression in his host's eyes. Or rather, the lack of expression, for the pupils which scrutinized him so keenly were bleak as the eyes of a dead creature. Colourless eyes. Chipped ice eyes. Eyes without the slightest warmth of human emotion.

'My dear Captain, how are you?' the Ice Man said. 'I'm Zarafiq . . . Mister Zarafiq.'

'Well, I'm bloody aggravated!' Trapp retorted, the pain of financial injury overcoming his uncharacteristic lack of poise. 'An' if you're head sheik of this bucket, then it's you that owes me fifteen hun . . . two thousand quid. F'r damages an' destruction of plant what was only on hire, so to speak.'

Mister Zarafiq held up an immaculate hand. 'I am desolate, dear Captain. Utterly desolate that employees of mine should have been so . . . so ill-advised in their manner of approaching you.'

'Yeah? Well, they're still approachin' Wullie,' Trapp said pointedly. 'Two at a time, down on your foredeck. They're kickin' the shit outa him!'

Mister Zarafiq registered horror and disillusionment. Except through his eyes, of course. 'Your first officer?'

He turned to one of the two seamen-gunmen standing impassively behind Trapp and snapped an order in Arabic. The man withdrew silently while Zarafiq shook a doleful head. 'One finds it so difficult to depend on hired help nowadays when we live in a world of violence. The molestation of your companion will cease immediately.'

'Mind you, it don't ackshully bother Wullie,' Trapp hastened to assure him. 'He's a tiger, y'see. Not frightened of nothin', he reckons . . . Not like them little Pakistani passengers I had. Before your employees decided they wus excess cargo?'

Mister Zarafiq had obviously plumbed the uttermost depths of distress. 'Ah, those poor unfortunate people,' he murmured dolefully. 'Innocent victims of man's inhumanity to man . . .'

'What you mean is that it's all come as a big surprise to you, naturally,' Trapp broke in dryly. 'An' that you di'n't know about the throat cuttin' an' murder an' that. Or that your boys was goin' to cost me two thou . . . two and a half thousand quid.'

'One finds such difficulty in controlling even one's own destiny,' reflected Mister Zarafiq helplessly. 'Therefore can one ever hope to be able to pre-ordain the path of life for others, Captain?'

'Cut the poor bastard's throat an' you've had a pretty good try at it,' Trapp argued reasonably. 'Come to that, you've managed a bit've rearranging my future right now.

What with sinking a good three thousand pounds' worth've boat, and a profitable business venture, right from under me.'

'Have a cigarette, my dear chap,' offered the distraught host. 'Or a Martini. A pleasantly chilled beer, perhaps? And do please excuse my not partaking of anything stronger than a small lemonade. Merely another cross we devout Moslems are called upon to bear.'

'An' that's the end of that conversation,' Trapp reflected savagely. 'Epitaph f'r three pathetic little victims; a hollow platitude, a crocodile tear . . . an' a glass of lemonade to wash away the taste of vomit.'

But he didn't say anything more. Because that was the moment when – apart from being a bigger liar and even more parsimonious than Edward Trapp himself – he realized precisely how dangerous and how ruthless a man Mister Zarafiq could be.

For there was a small wooden tray on Mister Zarafiq's desk; full of trivia such as elastic bands and paper clips and things. But there were other items also lying casually in that tray; items which shocked and disgusted even the world-wise and cynical Trapp.

Three rings. Three ordinary, rather worn gold finger-rings. Yet they proved beyond any doubt that at least one of Mister Zarafiq's allegedly unreliable employees was rather more conscientious and well trained than Mister Zarafiq apparently wished Trapp to believe. Whether it had been Fadel or the other injured man plucked from the burning wheelhouse before the *Last Hope* finally sank didn't matter; what *was* pertinent was the fact that one of them had dutifully brought those rings aboard as a prize for his chief, the Ice Man.

Trapp knew he'd seen them once before, if only briefly. For Trapp had a photographic eye for gold. Only once before, but not very long ago . . . on the fingers of three brown men as they struggled to climb aboard his Blackbird boat on the far side of the English Channel . . .

. . . but then Mister Zarafiq sipped his drink, tapped his

cigarette languidly against the side of the exquisite bronze ashtray before him, and said conversationally, 'Would you like to earn twenty-five thousand pounds, my dear chap?'

'Thirty,' Trapp growled automatically; still eyeing the rings with a growing and terrible anger.

Then he blinked, and forgot about the rings. Temporarily.

'Pardon?'

Mister Zarafiq smiled; a jolly, amused smile. 'Twenty-five thousand pounds sterling, Captain Trapp. I would be so grateful if you would accept it . . .

'. . . to take sole command of this ship. For a period not to exceed four months from tonight.'

Trapp sat down abruptly. He couldn't help it. Money had a strange effect on his locomotory system when it was discussed in large quantities, and twenty-five thousand pounds was liable to trigger a condition of near-paralysis.

His mind was spinning, too. Emotions and reactions tumbled headlong in a conglomeration of avarice, gleeful disbelief, apprehension and – over-riding all else – wary and justifiable cynicism. For Trapp had already learned not to trust the personable Mister Zarafiq. He wouldn't have trusted anyone, for that matter, who had polished nails and went about causing other people's throats to be slit and fellow businessmen's investments to founder; but Mister Zarafiq was even lower than that, because Mister Zarafiq had proved himself a big-time operator yet with the desiccated morality and the seedy, greedy rapacity of a gutter degenerate.

So what return would the same man, who so casually expropriated the pitiful legacies of three murdered souls, demand for the vast sum of twenty-five thousand pounds?

'I don't kill people delib'rately,' Trapp managed to caution eventually. 'Or traffic in drugs an' that. Mind you, for thirty grand it bears a bit've thinkin' about, certainly.'

'Twenty-five,' Mister Zarafiq corrected in a very emphatic manner. 'Please, my dear fellow, are we not decent, civilized men? Would we ever consider offering violence and . . . and misery to our brother human beings purely for personal gain?'

'Not f'r a measly twenty-seven an' a half thousand quid, we wouldn't,' Trapp confirmed, with precisely the correct mixture of outraged virtue and hypocritical togetherness.

'Twenty-*five* thousand, Captain.' Mister Zarafiq began to look a little annoyed and the finger-nails fluttered petulantly.

'Twenty-six?' probed Trapp tentatively.

Mister Zarafiq gestured resignedly to the Arab seaman still waiting impassively by the door. The man stepped across and hit Trapp behind the ear with the foresight of his gun. Trapp went over with a roar of black rage and agony while Zarafiq took another appreciative sip of delicately chilled lemonade.

'Twenty-five thousand pounds it will be, then. I am so glad you agree – negotiating terms can be such a protracted and unpleasant task unless one or other of the parties concerned is prepared to make concessions, don't you think?'

The conceding party blinked at the carpet through a haze of blood and an almost irresistible desire to launch himself across the desk there and then and the hell with the consequences. But he didn't. A levelled sub-machinegun suggested he shouldn't for one thing, and Trapp was nothing if not a pragmatist. But there was something else which held him back – apart from a fervent desire to earn twenty-six . . . no, twenty-five thousand pounds an' that was f'r sure – and that was an implacable resolution that he would square the account at some time in the not-too-far-distant future with this smoothly lethal Ice Man.

But not now. Not right away. Not until the books of Trapp International Enterprises were revealing a very satisfying profit.

With which resolve he hauled himself erect; couldn't quite conceal the look in his eyes which should, in itself, have made Mister Zarafiq a very unsettled man; so covered up by forcing a wry, sporting loser's grin.

'With your approach to negotiations, mister, you should've been a diplomat . . . what's the job?'

While he didn't miss the flicker of . . . something in the Ice Man's expression. Wasn't it when he used the term 'diplomat'? But the suave manner was back again, above the glass of lemonade.

'This ship is currently *en route* for Port Said, Captain. Once she arrives she will load a cargo of used construction equipment . . . bulldozers, tractors, earth-moving trucks, small tools . . . all originally purchased from the Egyptian Government after the completion of the Aswan Dam project.'

'Bound for?'

'Málaga. Spain.'

'And that's the voyage you want me to make with her?'

'Ostensibly . . . yes.'

Trapp raised a knowing eyebrow. 'Which means you have somethin' a bit different in mind?'

'Twenty-five thousand pounds is a great deal of money. I am sure you have already anticipated that your rather restricted period of employment as master of the *Kamaran* will be expected to take a somewhat . . . ah . . . unconventional course, so to speak?'

'So that's 'er name. Genuine, is it?'

Mister Zarafiq looked hurt. 'But of course, my dear chap. Highest Bureau Veritas classification; insured with Lloyds; registered in the port of Massawa . . .'

'Then how unconventional *is* your sort of unconventional, mister?'

Zarafiq held his glass to the light and studied it intently. 'Merely that I should not consider it desirable that you complete your passage to Málaga.'

Trapp frowned. 'Coffin ship, you mean. Scuttle 'er, then claim on insurance . . .?'

Then he hesitated suspiciously. '. . . except that would only make sense with a clapped-out rust bucket; over-valued an' with a falsely manifested cargo of junk. Yet this

Kamaran o' yours ain't no beauty, but she's still worth plenty – and accordin' to you she really will be loadin' a genuine cargo before she sails.'

The Ice Man seemed pleased. 'A most astute observation. Which is why the authorities should have no cause to probe for ulterior motives behind the loss of such a well-found ship. Simply another mystery of the sea; inexplicable, but all too common even today.'

Trapp wriggled uneasily; this was a proposal which mortally offended his sense of ethical commercial practice. 'But there ain't no profit in it either, f'r cryin' out loud! An' anyway, you know as well as I do that you could've found a dozen skippers in Port Said alone who'd sink 'er f'r the price of a case of booze – an' with most of 'em it'd be a genuine mistake any'ow.'

Zarafiq eyed his guest appraisingly; thoughtfully. Then he placed his glass on the desk and sat back. 'I think it is time for explanations, Captain. Regarding the *Kamaran*, my interest in her and, perhaps of more immediate concern to yourself, my reasons for wishing to hire your somewhat . . . ah . . . esoteric services.'

Trapp scratched his head absently and his hand came away smeared with blood. He said bleakly, 'It's always a good time, the present.'

'Firstly, you must understand that I am neither the owner of the *Kamaran* nor her cargo-to-be; that I am simply a business consultant appointed, rather like yourself, to manipulate the affairs of my current task-masters. What you might call a . . . a . . .'

'A fixer?' Trapp suggested artlessly.

'. . . an investment efficiency counsellor,' Mister Zarafiq corrected tightly.

'Ah!' said Trapp. With a very cynical leer.

'The world shipping market is, as you are perhaps aware, currently suffering its most serious economic depression since the Second World War . . .'

'Yeah, I do know,' Trapp confirmed pointedly. 'Some bastard keeps sinkin' them. An' you can't get more

36

depressed than when your boat's lyin' thirty fathoms under the English Channel, can yer?'

'. . . and consequently vessels such as this are becoming more and more unprofitable to maintain in service.'

'It's you Ayrabs at fault, mind,' Trapp supplemented reprovingly. 'Steadily shovin' up the price of bunker fuel . . .'

This time he *did* halt abruptly; for it wasn't only the glare in Zarafiq's eyes which suggested Trapp was pushing vindictiveness just a little too far – no. There was a definite tightening of the Ice Man's expression when he'd sardonically mentioned 'bunker fuel'. But why . . . why should a throw-away observation like that cause any reaction at all?

'This also means,' Zarafiq continued stiffly, 'that while the *Kamaran* has an insured value of some one and a half million pounds, her saleable worth on the open shipping market could be less than one-third of that figure.'

Whereupon Edward Trapp fell strangely thoughtful, and it hadn't only been the warning in his opponent's bleak gaze. Because Trapp had suddenly begun to understand how, with a little imagination, a one-million-pounds-plus capital investment could be re-circulated from a cost-hungry white elephant. And he also had the feeling that there was more to come; that Mister Zarafiq's counselling was very efficient indeed.

And he wasn't disappointed.

'Furthermore,' the Arab progressed with a rather more benign tone, now that he could see Trapp was a true appreciator of commercial genius, 'the cargo you will load belongs to the self-same group of business gentlemen – though naturally this common ownership has been well camouflaged by the use of several subsidiary holding companies. And that cargo in question has an immediate resaleable value of . . . oh, shall we say a further one million pounds?'

'You c'n say that kind've figure as often as you like,' Trapp murmured expansively. Just the mention of money

– that volume of money – was as balm to his wounds; a soporific to his simmering resentment.

Until he remembered the three gold finger-rings. And the shattered *Last Hope*, now gone for ever . . . and the fact that he'd already discovered he couldn't trust a single word the Ice Man so convincingly uttered.

'Except it's a bit academic – the value of the cargo,' he added searchingly. 'Seein' you don't figure on ever makin' a profit from that; not unless fish have a need f'r bulldozers.'

Mister Zarafiq smiled. It was a clever, self-congratulatory sort of smile with the slightest hint of patronage. 'But, my dear chap, you really do have such little faith in my capacity for intrigue. Surely you have noticed the great effort I have made to engage your own . . . ah . . . somewhat specialized services?'

'It had struck me.'

Then Trapp allowed conceit to override cynicism. 'Mind you, I gotter admit I have a lot of expertise. Which partic'lar accomplishment did you 'ave in mind?'

'Your intimate knowledge of the North African coast. I can think of no other man with a greater capacity for avoidance of curious authority.'

'You mean 'cause I keep out've the way of gunboats to stay in business.'

'You are too modest. You are the man who actually contrived to run circles around the might of the German Navy *and* wage a most successful war at the same time, some years ago. You are, in fact, a maestro in the arts of clandestine deception, Captain Trapp. I salute you.'

'An' you don't know the half of it, yer connivin', parsimonious fairy,' Trapp promised viciously to himself. Outwardly he merely offered a modest acknowledgement of his due, and a deprecatory shrug.

'Even as the top man in me field, I still can't help you cash in on a scuttled cargo – apart from claimin' one million quid's worth of insurance money for what you've lost anyway . . . can I?'

'You can. Because, sir, that cargo will not *be* on board when this ship goes to the bottom of the Mediterranean. In fact it has already been sold – by my principals, of course – to a most reprehensible syndicate of plant distributors based in the State of Gahman . . .'

'Ahhhhh!' breathed Trapp in unreserved admiration; finally appreciating how it was that Mister Zarafiq proposed to turn commercial adversity into a fiscal *tour de force*.

Even as the smooth and perfumed voice continued, '. . . your skills will be utilized to the full, Captain. In order to off-load that cargo in total secrecy at a pre-arranged rendezvous on the Gahman coast before you return to your original course line for Málaga . . .'

'. . . an' then scuttle 'er?'

'You have hit the eye of the bull, my friend. The *Kamaran* will go down empty and commercially worthless – yet still insured for a total of nearly three million pounds sterling.'

It was a pity that Mister Zarafiq had actually put it into words – three million pounds.

I mean . . . well . . . three million pounds. An' in sterling, at that.

It was probably that phrase more than any other which generated a vision within the mind of Edward Trapp; a barely-germinated seed – a seed as golden as if inspired by the touch of Midas himself – which promised to flourish into a money tree more prolific than any he had chanced upon since the gloriously piratical hey-dey of World War II . . .

. . . for Trapp had already conceived of the first glimmerings of how he could not only obtain his revenge on the abominable Ice Man, but also show a profit. All it required was a little more patience, and a little more co-operation.

He never even heard the warning bell this time; the one

that clanged in a positive hysteria of reproof as soon as he made that rash decision. But avarice had yet another psychosomatic manifestation in the body of Edward Trapp . . .

. . . for not only did it make him deaf – it also made him bloody stupid.

CHAPTER FOUR

And that was how Mister Zarafiq became a potentially endangered species; Gorbals Wullie became a temporary tiger; and how Edward Trapp unexpectedly became both master-designate of the motor vessel *Kamaran*, and a conflicting battle-ground for caution versus greed.

And – of much more importance to me – how I became involved yet again with Trapp; and virtually press-ganged into that lunatic voyage of mayhem and bloody skull-duggery . . .

Oh, not that I had been ensnared at the start, Lord, no. When that initial and typically macabre encounter in the English Channel was taking place I was still a long way away – homeward bound from Yokohama to Liverpool as master of my own ship; and Edward Trapp merely a thirty-year-old memory which never quite faded; a spectre who still insisted on swashbuckling and grumbling and penny-pinching and glowering from the nocturnal recesses of my nightmares on those nights before I finally slammed awake to stare blindly up at the deckhead above my berth, and remember.

Trapp. And Trapp's War.

It had been *my* bloody war too, f'r that matter . . .

But that was all in the past, thank God. Even the violent meeting between my phantom pirate and the Ice Man Zarafiq had taken place some time before – it was over a month later that I berthed my own ship stern-to in Port Said harbour and made my way by taxi to Red Sweet-water . . .

Actually its title – the Red Sweetwater Nightclub – was a bit of a misnomer. For a start it wasn't so much a nightclub as a degenerate hovel, while the only red in evidence was in the colour of the enticing lamp hanging above the door and the customers' blood spattered across the foyer, a legacy of the previous evening's jollifications.

In fact it was more . . . well . . . blue, really. By virtue of the subject matter of the films they showed continuously above the bar, and the live acts they offered either on the postage-stamp stage or – for a quite exorbitant surcharge – upstairs to those clients whose needs for gratification inclined more towards the physical than the purely voyeuristic.

And then there was the blue haze, of course, which substituted for oxygen; and the blue-veined breasts of the grossly writhing belly dancers. All intermixed with the blue-denim silhouettes of the multi-national seamen and resident bums and drop-outs who gaily contracted each other's anti-social diseases via the Red Sweetwater girls with drunken abandon.

There was even a sort of matching, mottled-blue tinge to the features of an Egyptian queer who was being discreetly garrotted with his own tie in a dark corner just as I entered, though nobody seemed all that concerned. Certainly the two French matelots he'd solicited were carrying out the act with minimal inconvenience to the adjacent tables; every care being taken to ensure that his convulsive kicks didn't reach anyone.

It was that sort of place, like I've said . . .

. . . which seemed to make it so very unnecessary. The consternation and unpleasantness that were caused. Just because I shot a couple of policemen.

I'd been at the bar for about half an hour before the man I was to meet came in. He levered his heavy torso on to the stool beside me without a word and wheezed asthmatically while I hoisted in the final moments of a cinematographic epic starring three ladies, two Japanese male contortionists, two desert mules, an Afghan wolfhound and a basketful of eels.

Well, I think they were Japanese. Though they could've been Philippinos, or even Chi . . .

'Getta fuckin' move on then,' the Fat Man grumbled anxiously.

'I'd like to,' I retorted, thinking about the film again. Then I remembered, with a shock of apprehension, the real reason for my being there and hooked my foot around the duffle bag beside me, sliding it towards him, concealed by the overhang of the bar counter. It was heavy, and it had already travelled all the way from Hong Kong hidden behind a false panel in my cabin.

It may have been my over-stimulated imagination but I could have sworn the whole place quietened as I did so. As if shadowy, anonymous watchers knew what was happening; could sense a very hot item was being passed.

Fat Man tried unsuccessfully to toe the merchandise from me; unsuccessful partly because his legs were too short to do more than wave fruitlessly in the air below the high stool, and partly because I kept my foot on the bag.

'The money,' I hissed, getting even more nervy. 'You've got to give me the *money* first, stupid!'

But what the hell. We were both amateurs at the game; even if I did pride myself on looking a bit like Humphrey Bogart, while Fat Man could have doubled as a grosser version of Sydney Greenstreet.

Clumsily he produced a newspaper-wrapped bundle which might have been anything if it hadn't been for the wad of green US dollar bills advertising themselves to the world through one tattered corner. By then my nerves were beginning to twang like the wire on a runaway windlass, because it certainly wasn't only imagination telling me we were attracting even more attention than the sweating, grinding torsos just commencing a new act on stage.

'Go on – TAKE it then,' my fellow conspirator urged with a note of stertorous hysteria while, at the same time, staring fixedly at the bottles behind the bar and pretending he didn't even know I was there.

I took a deep breath. This was it. This was the moment I'd been dreading ever since they gave me that bloody duffle bag and those rather enigmatic instructions back in Hong Kong . . .

Dimly I was aware of two virtually simultaneous movements, one on either side of me. The first was of a figure – several figures in fact – jerking erect in the deepest, darkest corner of the room. And of a voice, a chillingly reminiscent voice, blurting incredulously, 'Number One! Stap me blind in me seaboots if it ain't the brassbounder hisself . . .'

The other diversion was from the door. A more violent diversion. Uniforms. Shrill protests from the Egyptian bouncers; the *crack* of a nightstick against someone's skull . . . more shrill Arabic and the scuffle of bodies being thrust aside. A tidal wave of peaked caps and white belts and khaki drill advancing towards me . . .

. . . I deliberately placed my hand on the bundle of dollar bills.

Just as a spotlamp snapped on; freezing me in the act; illuminating my guilt for every befuddled eye blinking through the blue haze of Red Sweetwater.

And a second voice – a well-spoken but faintly accented voice – snapped in unmistakable triumph, 'You are under arrest, Captain Miller. Please stay exactly as you are.'

This time there was no reciprocal movement from the group at the rear; it was almost as if they'd never been. As though the very glimpse of police uniforms had caused them to dissolve once again, and with professional adroitness.

I stared blindly into the glare of accusation. There was the faintest glimmer of a gold-braided cap above it, but nothing else. Even the background clamour had evaporated under the frustrated heavy breathing of the interrupted floor-show participants, allied with the asthmatic nervousness of the fat man beside me.

I said shakily, 'So who the hell are you, then? An' what's

the charge, mister?'

'Colonel of Police Rahman al Sidqi, Prohibited Drugs Division. I think you are already aware of the charge, Captain.'

Fat Man squealed, 'Awwwww *shit!*' and pulled out a gun. He couldn't even do that right though, and fell off the stool in a frantically waving pudge of arms and legs. There was a ·38-calibre explosion from beside al Sidqi – suggesting my fellow Briton wasn't the only bloke to get trigger-happy in the Red Sweetwater affair – and Fat Man slammed back against the bar with an expression of shock on his multi-chinned features . . .

. . . and then all hell let loose.

Someone directed a very French expression of dis-approval and a metal chair towards the nearest policeman. Next to him a knife, with a German seaman on one end of it and an Egyptian constable on the other – the pointed one – flashed in the glare of the spotlamp. A lithe and ebony-skinned girl darted in a nude, rising scream through a suddenly very ugly mob of anti-establishment visitors to Port Said.

And another voice – another equally familiar nightmare from my past – began screeching vindictively, 'Kill the bastids! Scunner they poofy wog polis bastids . . . Ah'm a tiger, a reg'lar tiger, lads, an' ah'm tellin' yous tae kill them poofy fuzzes, so ah am . . .'

Fat Man gave up trying to support himself against the bar and began to slide to the floor. I snatched the gun out of his nerveless fingers just as most of the Colonel's Prohibited Drugs Division disappeared under a welter of pummelling hostility . . . but then, nobody likes the Egyptian police; not even the bloody Egyptians.

The colonel was still on his feet, though. As well as the adjacent gleam of sergeant's stripes and the ·38 police special below them; both moving determinedly towards me.

'Look OUT, MILLERRRRR.' Another disembodied

warning from the secret shadows.

I glimpsed another trooper closing in on my starboard side, followed by another with a swinging baton and a glare of black rage . . .

. . . I fired convulsively. Twice.

Dimly I became aware of someone going out through a window in a clamour of shattering glass. Simultaneously the trooper with the nightstick was being pulled down by a brace of compatriot villains with old scores to settle. They were delightedly stamping on his face as more policemen charged through the entrance doors. And more; an' bloody more.

I still didn't move; simply staring disconcertedly at the bodies of Colonel al Sidqi and his sergeant lying in contorted submission under the smoking barrel of Fat Man's revolver. My revolver now.

While, equally ominously, the majesty of the Law was beginning to win.

The German knife sailor screaming in agony as three Egyptian batons homed in on him as one, shattering both his arms. A Frenchman on his knees, spitting blood, teeth and Gallic epithets, while another squad of khaki-clad constabulary kicked him into a grovelling, pleading hideosity.

And even more reinforcements. Sirens . . . Blue again – blue flashing emergency strobes outside in the street; playing through the open doors and across the intently struggling mob . . . I spun round with the fear acrid in my throat . . .

. . . to meet the cavernous barrel of a twelve-bore riot gun levelled straight at my head. I seemed to be one involuntary scream away from having my brains sprayed all over the Nightclub Red Sweetwater . . .

Just before the lights went out. Almost as though someone had pulled the Red Sweetwater's main power switch.

And a disembodied hand yanked me – and the duffle bag – clear across the bar and through a shrieking hysteria of

46

milling belly dancers. And through a rear exit, into the night.

We must have run for a good twenty minutes – myself and my two shadowy pilots – before we finally ground to a rasping, lung-tortured halt.

I didn't have a clue where we were; it was still as dark as the innards of the Cheops Pyramid. Port Said's side streets do tend to cloak all nocturnal movement with a discretion born out of centuries of clandestine depravity. Only the occasional reed lantern of a middle watch silversmith or basket weaver or ox butcher had flashed briefly across the galloping figures of my escorts as we passed, like fairway buoys against the hulls of some outward-bound flotilla.

It didn't matter though. I'd already guessed, with cold certainty, at the identities of my puffing Samaritans. Those long-ago familiar voices raised above the opening stages of the battle of Red Sweetwater had established beyond any shred of doubt that the dead really could be resurrected; that nightmares really could become fact.

I still felt the shock of it, all the same. Whatever I'd been led to expect when I'd originally agreed to perform that crazy charade back there, it certainly hadn't been anything quite as outlandish as this.

When the bulkier of the two figures stepped forward so that the glow from a nearby brazier fell across his ageless, craggy features; and smiled an all-too-well-remembered leer of virtuous reproval.

And said, 'Evenin', mister. So who's been a naughty boy, then?'

He looked just the same as ever, did Trapp. As if thirty intervening years of maritime villainy had glanced off him like breakers under the bows of an unsinkable ship.

It also proved I had been right all the time; that all those sleepless nights had well and truly justified my uncertainty about whether he and Gorbals Wullie really had been dragged down along with all the rest of that insanitary, buccaneering crew of homicidal tramps, in the whirl-

47

pooling wreckage of His Majesty's Warship *Charon*; indisputably the most unorthodox and appalling mistake ever to fly the White Ensign of the Royal Navy.

Oh, not that the Royal Navy had agreed with me at the time, mind you. After all, Trapp did help them win the battle of the Mediterranean, even though his motives had been rather more pecuniary than patriotic. They'd even awarded him a medal for it – or they'd given me the medal in actual fact, which had been the only nice part of the war as far as I'd been concerned, seeing it was posthumous, and simply accepted on his behalf.

Except that it hadn't been, had it? Because he bloody well hadn't been, had he . . . if you see what I mean.

'You're dead,' I accused pleadingly; hopefully. 'You died thirty years ago, Trapp. You an' that little Scotch ferret beside you.'

The ferret stepped forward, too. And he really did look like a ferret; a ferret with a three-day growth and a greasy cloth cap.

'Ah'm no' dead,' Gorbals Wullie announced reassuringly. 'Ah'm a tiger, Mister Miller, sir.'

''Is brain's dead,' Trapp admitted. Then he thought a bit and supplemented, 'Well, not dead, ackshully. More still-born really, seein' how it never worked in the first place.'

But he'd always been a stickler for accuracy, had Edward Trapp. I began to feel I was smothering as all my old apprehensions flooded back with the realization that not only was Trapp still alive, but that he hadn't changed one iota. Two ambulances went clanging past the end of the alley, heading towards the Red Sweetwater, and it occurred to me then to flag one down, climb aboard, and claim immunity as a latent casualty of war.

Because, you see, I was different. Quite special in a screwed-up sort of way. Oh, admittedly there were a great many men with thirty-year-old ghosts inside their heads; victims of battle stress – Trapp himself was one, come to that. But in those instances their mental scars had been inflicted largely by enemy action, whereas I had suffered

48

my twitches and traumas from a much more exclusive source . . . from my supposed allies.

In my case all those bombs and bullets and *Kriegsmarine* torpedoes hadn't terrorized me any more or less than the next British seaman. No, it had been all the times between attacks that had caused my psychological wounds; my aggravations had been generated not so much through battling with Hitler's navy as against my bloody own. Against a certain Lieutenant Commander Edward Trapp, RNR, and the sadistic ill-fortune that had made him my commanding officer . . .

I got a grip on myself. 'I suppose I ought to thank you for getting me out of there,' I muttered grudgingly. 'I guess that's a favour I owe you.'

'Two favours, Number One,' Trapp corrected firmly. 'It wus me an' Wullie here what pulled you out've the water an' left you on that bit o' hatch cover after the old *Charon* went down, remember?'

I remembered. I'd often wondered about it later. Though maybe he was wrong when he called it a favour; they hadn't been particularly good or successful times for me since.

'Don't call me "Number One",' I snapped, feeling the old irritation coming back as easily as if we'd never parted. 'I'm a shipmaster in my own right, Trapp. I've been one for twenty years, dammit.'

'Not now, you're not,' he pointed out shyly. 'Every fuzz in the United Ayrab Republic'll be lookin' for you over the sights o' a gun. You go anywhere near your old ship an' you're good f'r thirty years' hard inna wog jail . . . Number One.'

'Aye, but yous is in the shit an' that's a fact, Mister Miller, sir,' Gorbals Wullie confirmed somewhat unnecessarily. 'Yous is a marked man . . . whit's in the bag then?'

I blinked. His abrupt change of tack had caught me off balance, then I saw what he was holding up so curiously – it was my duffle bag. I grabbed it and snarled, 'Mind your own bloody business, sailor!'

'Heroin?' Trapp speculated with the slightest inflection of genuine disapproval; but I was forced to admit he'd always had his principles. I grimly refused to answer.

'Opium, then . . . Maryjooanna?'

'It's nothing, Trapp.'

'It wus enough to start a riot, mister. An' to kill a couple o' policemen for. An' who was your fat mate before they shot him too, eh?'

'I'd never seen him before in my life,' I retorted truthfully.

'That don't quite answer the question,' countered Trapp astutely, then swung as a police jeep with the regulation-issue flashing blue lamp careered across the alleyway exit and vanished. When he turned back to face me he seemed to have forgotten all about the bag.

'Now I *am* a shipmaster,' he volunteered with an immensely superior smirk.

'How d'you know?' I challenged spitefully. 'You haven't seen it for a couple of hours. The kind of rust bucket you sail in, it could have sunk at its berth by now.'

He didn't seem to mind a bit; he simply grinned and looked quite pleased, as though he hadn't had a good insult since . . . well, since *I* last sailed with him.

'Bureau Veritas classification, mister. Six an' a half thousand tons gross o' shiny paint an' sweet-runnin' machinery . . . Name's the *Kamaran*. I'm sailin' soon as I've finished loading. For Málaga.'

'That's in Spain, ye ken,' Wullie supplemented helpfully once again. Trapp cuffed him across the starboard ear with a growl.

''E knows that, limpet brain. Mister Miller's a captain too, remember?'

Then he corrected himself with a sideways glance at me. '. . . or he was a cap'n. Until he signed hisself off articles by startin' that gunfight back at the Sweetwater corral.'

I hefted the bag and turned away. Trapp said doubtfully,

'Where d'you think you're goin'?'

'On the run,' I answered tightly. 'The Egyptian authorities are likely to be offensive enough without your bloody help.'

'Ye've nae chance, ah'm tellin' ye. Ye're doomed, Mister Miller; doomed never tae get oot o' this land o' the pyramids an' the sphincters . . .'

'Shut up!' Trapp snarled almost absently. But he'd been saying that to Gorbals Wullie for over thirty years and it wasn't so much an order as a habit. He rubbed the side of his nose and fixed me with the honest, open gaze of a spider inviting a fly to lunch.

'Mind you, there is one way you jus' might get out o' here, me bucko . . .'

'Inna box,' Wullie persisted. 'Deid, an' inna wooden box stowed down the freezer hold.'

'. . . I'm still signin'-on crew for the *Kamaran* . . .' Trapp continued undeflected.

'No.' I forestalled him. 'No way, Trapp. And that's my final word.'

'. . . there's still a berth open f'r a chief officer . . .?'

I began walking towards the end of the alleyway, and the bright lights and the searching police cars – and the apparent promise of thirty years in an Egyptian labour camp. Even that prospect had more attraction than sailing again with Edward Trapp. It wouldn't be quite so inevitably lethal, for a start; and I wouldn't have as many arguments with the guards.

There was another reason, too, why I didn't dare accept right away. I couldn't afford to let him see what really was in my bag.

'I got half a dozen seamen's discharge books what only needs a photgraph ter make 'em genuine. A bit o' hair dye an' a week's growth o' beard an' you could call in at the local police station an' they wouldn't know you.'

The hypocrisy in his voice was positively honeyed. Edward Trapp had always been a man to extract the last advantage from any situation . . . until he came up against someone as bloody-minded and stubborn as himself.

And then he admitted he had.

'Awwwww, SOD YOU!' he yelled at the top of his voice. 'Keep yer bloody duffle bag, mister. From now on I coul'n't care bloody less what's innit . . .'

I stopped walking, and smiled a secret smile.

It was the first time I'd ever won a game of bluff with Captain Edward Trapp.

We sneaked aboard the *Kamaran* an hour later. It wasn't particularly difficult; pretty well every policeman and every spare floodlight in the Nile Delta had already been positioned round my previous ship on the other side of the basin.

I remember standing there on that strangely inhospitable deck, and blinking across at my old command with a feeling of empty sadness. I knew that whatever happened from now on, I would never take that particular ship to sea again. I'd really sunk to the bottom of the ocean-going barrel now, even though there had been a little more to my meeting with Trapp than pure coincidence . . .

. . . but anyway – that was how I became chief officer of an already doomed vessel called the *Kamaran*.

And how, despite already having fought Trapp's War, I was now miserably preparing myself to fight Trapp's Peace.

Oh, there was one more task I had to complete, even before I could examine the admittedly rather pleasant cabin I'd now taken over . . . It only took a few minutes of thought to discover a suitable place. Quickly I removed a pile of old newspapers lying in the bottom of the wardrobe, and unscrewed the false plywood base. Yes, there was just enough room.

Then I opened the duffle bag – the one which had generated so much discomfort among the clients and visitors to Red Sweetwater; and which had been so grudgingly abandoned by a covetous Trapp – and removed the only object which it contained.

It fitted very neatly into the hiding place I'd found. Once the newspapers were piled roughly on top it would never attract a second glance.

That small short-wave radio transmitter. The one the Royal Navy had issued me with, way back in Hong Kong.

CHAPTER FIVE

I skulked aboard the *Kamaran*, virtually living in my cabin, for six whole days until the cargo loading was virtually complete. By the end of it I was hairy enough to have passed myself off as a yeti, never mind the Australian-born Bert Cooper that Trapp's forged seaman's discharge papers said I was.

At least I hoped the book was forged. Because if it wasn't, then the mind boggled at why the real Bert Cooper hadn't any further need for it. I didn't risk asking Trapp – there were rare but carefully selected occasions when he could be unsettlingly honest.

On the seventh day I ventured on deck. To meet what could be loosely described as 'The Crew' . . .

It was as if I'd never left Red Sweetwater. Nearly every pugilistic, hard-bitten face which scowled moronically back at me from the muster line was already vaguely familiar. The last time I'd seen them was when they, and half the Egyptian riot squad, had been kickin' the sawdust out've each other back at the brothel.

'Lovely boys,' Trapp offered approvingly, even proudly, with a proprietary sweep of one great paw. 'Salt o' the earth, them. Every one with a record long as yer arm . . . part o' the contract, see. That I wus allowed to hand-pick the best blokes f'r the job.'

I swung on him immediately. 'Contract? Job . . .? I understood this was to be a straightforward voyage, Trapp . . .'

He developed a sudden coughing fit to change the subject, and hurriedly yanked the nearest man out of the line like a horse trader displaying his wares.

'Er, this is Choker Bligh, your bosun. Say 'allo to Mister

Mille . . . Mister Cooper, Choker, lad.'

The bosun spat on the deck between my feet and growled, 'Fuck you, mate! An' don't try givin' *me* no soddin' orders.'

Trapp urged me aside before I could lash out. 'He likes you,' he assured me solemnly. 'I c'n tell that right away. An' anyway, Choker's even more obligin' when he's drunk – an' 'e's drunk most've the time . . .'

The next for introductions looked like a puddle of oil wearing an Egyptian fez.

'Maabud somethin' or other. Chief engineer.'

The puddle of oil grovelled horizontally, leaving greasy splotches wherever he'd made contact with the deck. Trapp eventually kicked him and growled, 'Gerrup, mister. Mind you, he don't 'ave much personality, but a lotta experience. Fourteen years as chief engineer on the *Cairo Flyer* f'r a start.'

'That's a funny name for a ship,' I muttered bemusedly.

'That's because it wus a railway engine,' Trapp retorted with devastating logic. 'And the lumpy-lookin' guy with the scar an' the hare lip next to 'im – he's yer second mate. Name o' Spew . . . Dan'l Spew.'

I stared. Somehow, somewhere, I had to find something that could establish beyond reasonable doubt that Mister Spew had, at least at some time, been a human being.

'Is he qualified – for the job?'

'Outa the top drawer, mate. Two suspected murders; a bagful o' grievous bodily harms; three rapes; couple o' racecourse jobs . . .'

'I meant seagoing-wise,' I snarled desperately. 'As a bridge watchkeeper.'

Trapp nodded violently. 'Christ, yes. He even took a sort o' correspondence course in navigashun once, only 'e di'n't get too far with it.'

I had to ask why. It was something I just knew I had to do.

'Why didn't Mister Spew get very far with his correspondence course, Captain?'

'Because 'e can't read, Mister Mate. Or write, come ter that.'

I began to walk away again; it was getting to be a habit. Trapp's voice – still as nauseatingly persuasive as ever – floated astern of me, enumerating the other virtues of Second Officer Spew.

''E's gotter good pair o' eyes, mind you. Well, *one* of 'em is; the one what didn't get the acid innit . . . an' a lovely nature when you gets ter know 'im . . .'

There was one more thing I had to do before I left the *Kamaran*'s depraved complement and made my gloomy way topsides to view the bridge.

As I passed the truculent Bosun Bligh I nodded in the friendliest possible manner – and then kicked him as hard as I could in those parts which made places like Red Sweetwater his favourite form of recreation. I had to do it hard; I knew I wouldn't get a second chance before he dismantled me rivet by rivet. Then I continued kicking him as he sprawled on the deck until fatigue brought me to a puffing halt.

I waited until he'd stopped retching, then barked grimly, 'Rest assured I have no intention of *trying* to give you orders, sailor. I bloody *will* give you orders . . . an' you shall carry 'em OUT!'

'F**@£*''&****!' Choker Bligh acknowledged, much to Trapp's obvious delight.

'Ye see – he *does* like yer, mister! Di'n't I tell you 'e likes you then . . .?'

The *Kamaran*'s bridge deck was like the rest of her – functional but unimaginative; a typical product of an almost dying age of mass-produced general cargo ships. Now the tendency was towards specialization and economy; containerization and even larger carrying capacities. The *Kamaran* was too small, required too many men to run and maintain her; but she was still a well-found vessel and the more I thought about it the uneasier I became.

Because there was a mystery in the air on that bridge. It just wasn't Trapp's kind of ship – nothing was Trapp's kind of ship other than the sort which even the breakers' yards wouldn't touch as there's no profit in demolishing rust. So how had he come to command her and, even more unsettlingly, why . . . ?

. . . but perhaps I should explain – about my genuinely disconcerting meeting with a ghost; and about the radio and the subterfuge, and the fat man who got himself so ostentatiously blown away in Red Sweetwater.

The only snag in attempting to do that is that I didn't really understand 'why' myself. I simply did not know the underlying reasons for my being aboard the *Kamaran* in the first place other than as a somewhat confused undercover agent with the task of reporting her daily positions to some obscure Royal Navy station with the call sign of Charlie Tango Wun Fife and . . . well, to wait for orders.

Oh, I was aware of my own motives for having accepted the proposition first raised by those two naval officers back in Hong Kong a few weeks ago; the ones with the Security Department identity cards and the wheedling blarney of the recruiting office. Psychologically they'd selected the perfect time – my already being so disenchanted with the monotony of driving the same slab-sided container ship along the identical maritime taxi route I'd been covering for the past ten years, that I'd have considered any prospect short of suicide as a merciful release.

And I have to admit a lot of my unpreparedness was my own fault. I should have been far more persistent in following up their vague references to 'Britain's closest interests at stake . . .' and 'threat to national security, old boy . . .' but I hadn't been. No more than I really pursued the reasons why they considered *me*, a very ordinary master mariner, as being eminently suited for implanting as a . . . well . . . a spy, I suppose. Aboard some ship called the *Kamaran* carrying certain earthmoving equipment on behalf of a certain Mister Zarafiq; but to a rather more

57

doubtful destination, perhaps.

So I'd gratefully accepted the challenge, content, simply, to trust in God and my Queen and to report back to Charlie Tango. Apart from anything else a little Middle Eastern freighter loaded with bulldozers and picks and shovels was hardly likely to offer a threat even to me, never mind to Britain's national security; it had to be an intriguing cruise, a little bit of spurious excitement to brighten a dull career; a temporary relaxation from the responsibilities of command as an added bonus.

Dammit, but I'd been so taken by the prospect that I hadn't even voiced my doubts regarding the theatrical manner in which they'd proposed to infiltrate me into the world of subterfuge and undercover watch-keeping . . . about the Red Sweetwater ploy which had involved the co-operation of the Egyptian authorities, the appalling acting of a rather portly British Army intelligence major and the – to my mind somewhat over-melodramatic – use of a revolver loaded with blanks. Again, with total naïveté, I'd simply accepted the Navy's assurance that something would happen; that someone would contact me.

And by God they'd been right about that! The only small point they'd omitted to mention was that the factor guaranteeing *my* particular suitability for infiltration, was to be the resurrection of Edward bloody Trapp. But they'd also known that I wouldn't even have considered the job had I been forewarned of that possibility.

Which, in its turn, made me wonder what else the Royal Navy knew about the *Kamaran* but hadn't told me . . .

. . . but that was the moment when Trapp, flanked by the inevitable Gorbals Wullie, arrived at the top of the bridge ladder. With a feeling of something less than enthusiasm, I took the opportunity of performing the one last task outstanding before I was committed to becoming a fully-integrated and genuine pirate . . .

He noticed the duffle bag I'd brought aboard as soon as his beady eyes rose above deck level. I knew he would; apart from Trapp having a magnetic affinity towards

anything he considered might be either valuable or illegal –
preferably both – I'd also made a point of casually leaving it
where he was bound to trip over it anyway.

You see, I'd already learned that Trapp hadn't changed a
bit. The moment was bound to come when, by hook or by
crook, he would make an unashamedly devious attempt to
discover what really had precipitated the battle of Red
Sweetwater – but that was the one thing I couldn't risk him
finding out, seeing it wasn't anything like Trapp thought it
was, and was now hidden in my cabin tuned to a classified
frequency.

I also knew, however, that Edward Trapp had one
particular weakness which I could use to my advantage: he
simply couldn't resist the opportunity to become the most
hypocritical, holier-than-thou preacher there ever was. Or
initially anyway – before he went ahead and did precisely
whichever villainy had formed in his protagonist's mind in
the first place.

'It *is* drugs, i'n't it, mister?' he growled disapprovingly,
glance positively probing whatever secrets were held by
that innocuous canvas bag.

I pretended complete disinterest. 'You agreed, Trapp.
To mind your own business. Now, about the voyage; do we
have a full folio of corrected charts and a . . .'

Trapp and Gorbals Wullie moved a little closer to the
bag. 'Ah'll put ma money on it bein' drugs, onyway,' the
little seaman agreed, eyes beginning to glint like a rat's
caught in a spotlamp.

'You 'aven't *got* any money, stupid!' Trapp pointed out
contemptuously. 'You spent all yer allowance on that big
black wrestler lady up at Sweetwater las' night.'

'. . . and a set of sailing directions?' I persisted.

'Drugs,' Trapp tutted virtuously. 'I'm disappointed in
you, mister. Drugs is a wicked thing ter smuggle, an' you
bein' such a straight bloke when you wus young.'

'Forget it. Let's concentrate on the passage plan, Trapp.'

'. . . an' f'r money, too.'

'Aye, Captin, the things a man'll stoop tae, jus' f'r

money.' Wullie shook his scrofulous head in the sadness of utter disillusionment. By now they were both within an avaricious hair's breadth of diving for the bag and the great unveiling.

'. . . Admiralty Lists of Lights?' I insisted futilely.

'Ohh the misery; the 'uman suffering what can be caused by them that gets their hands on a bag o' drugs,' Trapp admonished, with tears of near-revulsion at how low a man could sink. 'Oh the wickedness o' it all; the . . . the *profit* in it . . .'

I hesitated, looked suddenly like a lost soul trying desperately to become aware of The Light.

'I never thought of it that way,' I muttered uneasily. 'Maybe you're right. Maybe I shouldn't hang on to it just for my own selfish gain.'

'You'll feel a lot better if you gets rid o' the guilt, matey,' Trapp urged, forcing his hand out to take upon himself the cancer which spawned within my duffle bag.

'Gie it *up*, Mister Miller, sir,' Wullie encouraged devoutly. 'Och but the relief ye'll feel once ye dinnae hae the worry of all yon valuable . . . all yon evil hard stuff on yer conscience, an' that's a fact.'

I picked up the bag, and drew a deep and saintly breath of deliverance.

'Thank you, both of you,' I whispered humbly. 'For guiding me back towards the path of righteousness . . .'

. . . and then I dropped the bag clear over the side of the bridge; right down into the inky depths of Port Said harbour. It disappeared for ever, with hardly a splash, but that was probably because of the heavy shackle I'd placed in it a few minutes before.

Trapp did make a few more comments, but I don't think they were particularly constructive. I felt they also tended towards being a little less than congratulatory, considering he'd just successfully rehabilitated a sinner.

Discreetly I retreated from the *Kamaran*'s bridge deck, leaving an inexplicably embittered preacher to kick his fellow gospeller all around the paint-shiny wheelhouse, trying to pretend Gorbals Wullie was me.

I should have known it couldn't last. It was actually a little later that same afternoon when I ran clean out of satisfaction.

I'd ventured back up to the chartroom after Gorbals Wullie had limped petulantly away, and spent a couple of hours laying off our courses for Málaga. Trapp had been there for most of the time, grumbling and muttering and fiddling with irrelevant things, but he hadn't said a word directly to me; only occasionally bellowing ill-tempered invective at Bosun Bligh and the unbelievably grotesque figure of Second Officer Spew as they struggled to supervise the loading of our deck cargo of giant bulldozers.

Then I noticed the Arabs.

Oh, not that the fact that they were Arabs was particularly odd in itself; one does tend to meet rather a lot of them around the Middle East. But these boys were different; they were very hard-looking Arabs indeed.

For a start they weren't working or anything; simply lounging in a huddle at the after end of the boat deck and watching the loading operation. Obviously not part of the stevedoring complement.

Yet they weren't part of the crew either. For one thing they looked clean; for another they didn't wear clothes looking like gear robbed from a mortuary after an air crash into a swamp. Expensive, they were, in lightweight linen and with ominously well-tailored bulges just about where a shoulder holster could be imagined.

There were five of them altogether. A point which caused me considerable unease was the way that one of them – a tall, sardonic-looking Arab with his arm in a sling – seemed to turn quite often and stare bleakly up at the bridge – up at Trapp, in fact – with a look of barely-veiled threat.

He gave the impression of being the man in charge. But of what? I knew one thing for sure – I didn't feel comfortable turning my back on them, not even for the few moments it took to corner a morose and embittered Trapp out on the wing.

Even after he did bring himself to speak to me it was only to go on about the bloody duffle bag, and his imagined loss of revenue.

'Yeah? Well what about all that misery and human suffering you were lecturing me about?' I was forced to counter eventually, before he would drop the subject.

'Wot about all *my* bloody misery an' sufferin', mister? An' Wullie's?'

'Gorbals Wullie hasn't got the mental capacity to worry about tomorrow's breakfast, never mind loss of profits, like you. *He* wasn't suffering over what was in my bag, Trapp.'

''E wus after I'd finished beltin' 'im around the ship . . .'

'What about those Arabs on the boat deck?' I finally cut in. 'Who are they, and why are they aboard, huh?'

He shuffled a bit then, and looked shifty. 'They're jus' passengers. Employees of a guy called Zarafiq; sort o' representatives of the owners in a way. Their head sheik is a guy called Fadel – the one with the funny arm.'

I saw the look of . . . was it satisfaction in his eye, but didn't understand it and felt faintly relieved with the rest of the explanation. 'So presumably they're going all the way to Málaga with us, eh?'

He wasn't really listening; just staring down at the oddly sinister group with what had gradually turned to a more worried, almost anxious expression.

'Where's Málaga?' he asked absently.

'In Spain f'r . . . our destination, Trapp. Málaga's the port of discharge for the *Kamaran*'s cargo, according to you.'

'What cargo?' he muttered even more remotely. And that was when I suddenly began to shiver. I'd seen that look of introspective villainy too many times before to have any illusions left.

I grabbed him, swinging him to face me guiltily.

'Trapp,' I snarled vengefully. 'Trapp, you double-dealing, bent-as-an-Irish-corkscrew, parsimonious bastard. The time has come for you an' me to have a long and candid talk . . .'

'. . . so that's all there is to it, mate,' he finished half an hour later. 'All we gotter do is nip in the boats; watch the old *Kamaran* go down by the 'ead; I gets paid the other half o' me contract; Zarafiq's happy . . . an' you're all on a handsome bonus.'

'That's all?' I echoed weakly. 'We only have to offload a whole cargo in a place we aren't even supposed to visit. Then scuttle this ship in the middle of the Mediterranean; and *then* convince the authorities we never went anywhere off our course line in the first bloody place . . .'

'That's all. More or less.'

I glowered at him searchingly. He looked far too innocent still; much too saintly.

'More or less . . . Trapp. What are you still covering up, Trapp? TRAPP?'

He shuffled again and examined his exploded baseball boots intently. I swung him around and shoved my face hard into his, eyeball to eyeball.

'What . . . are . . . you . . . bloody . . . concealing?'

I was half-way down the bridge ladder when he'd finished explaining *that* part; ostensibly *en route* for the gangway, the nearest police station, and thirty years' hard labour.

'What are you goin' for, mate?' he called anxiously. 'I told yer the truth, di'n't I? Jus' like you wanted.'

I stopped. Only for a minute, mind you. And only then because not even I, with all my knowledge of Edward Trapp, could quite hoist in the enormity of the enterprise his crooked brain had spawned on this particular occasion.

'You have told me, Trapp, that this mysterious Mister Zarafiq has paid you ten thousand pounds . . .'

His eyes flickered a bit guiltily at that and I knew I'd already caught him out, but it didn't matter; I'd no desire to share on a percentage basis anyway.

'. . . to offload the cargo to some secret purchasers, at

some equally secret rendezvous in Gahman, before you actually sink the ship. And because, for some inexplicable reason, Zarafiq finds it difficult to trust you, he has placed five professional gunmen aboard to make bloody certain you do what he's paying you to do . . .'

'Yeah, but . . .'

'Shut *up*, Trapp!'

I was aware of my voice cracking in fury, but I didn't care; I just had to get the whole lunatic swindle clear in my own mind before I opted out and back to the dull, honest world of containerships and ordinary people and maybe a few, revitalized nightmares.

'But ten thousand quid isn't good enough for you, is it, Trapp? Because now you tell me that not only have you already taken Zarafiq's advance payment . . . but that you have ALSO sold the cargo to a *second* bunch of crooks – to some of your own villainous mates – which means that now you intend to deliver it to *another* secret rendez-bloody-vous; this one somewhere along the North African coast before Zarafiq's place . . .'

'. . . an' sink the *Kamaran* before I'm due at Zarafiq's illegal destination too, mind,' Trapp argued reasonably. 'I mean, well, when she's scuttled he ain't got no way of knowin' I already got rid of the cargo, has he? So all I'm proposin' is to use his idea, only divert a little more of the boodle into me own pocket.'

'You can't. He'll never believe you, Trapp.'

'Why not? He expects the insurers to believe the *Kamaran* sunk 'erself by accident, don't he? All I'm doin' is the same thing but a bit earlier in the trip.'

I still hesitated on the ladder. The trouble with all Trapp's double-crossing schemes was that they seemed so bloody logical, so convincing. Then I remembered the Arab, Fadel, and that look of promise he'd directed towards Trapp; and the rest of his boys, and the bulges under the shoulder blades, and the cold professionalism.

'And what about Zarafiq's hoods, Trapp? D'you really think they're going to let you get away with it?'

'Aw, they're only Ayrabs,' Trapp dismissed scornfully. 'They don't 'ave the brain o' Gorbals Wullie between 'em. They wouldn't know one bit o' North Africa from Piccadilly Circus, they wouldn't. And when it comes to abandonin' the *Kamaran*, there's always the chance of an accident happenin'; a lifeboat fall partin' maybe, or the ladder they're using's gonna carry away sudden . . .'

He was still following me, accompanied now by an equally ingratiating Gorbals Wullie, even after I'd actually descended the gangway and was walking determinedly along the quay and away from the bloody *Kamaran*.

I'd have gone, too – Royal Navy or no Royal Navy. Clear out of Trapp's life again; only this time for ever and ever.

Well, I would if it hadn't been for the Chinamen, anyway.

The ones who kidnapped us.

CHAPTER SIX

I didn't even notice the smart launch at first. The one moored alongside the wharf ahead of the *Kamaran*'s looming bow.

I didn't particularly register the men grouped irresolutely beside it either, as if they didn't quite know what to do next – until they turned to see Trapp bearing down on them in voluble pursuit of me, and suddenly their not-so-inscrutable expressions cleared as their immediate problem appeared to have resolved itself.

Because the delicate task of kidnapping a shipmaster is made much simpler when that master actually comes ashore from the ship in question, and marches straight into your arms. Which was precisely what Trapp, still escorted by a frantically hobbling Gorbals Wullie, was doing. Presumably that early-warning sense of his had once again been overwhelmed by his anxiety to argue further with me.

He'd nearly come abeam of me by the time we'd steamed abreast of the Chinamen. All they needed to do was to step forward, present the muzzles of two not-particularly-discreetly-held sub-machineguns, and suggest invitingly, 'You all get into fligging boat, chop, chop.'

'Bugger OFF!' Trapp roared absently, sweeping both men aside with a mighty thrust of his paw and carrying on regardless.

Then he stopped; and Gorbals Wullie stopped. And I stopped too, rooted to the spot, as we heard the unmistakable snick of machinegun cocking handles being drawn back to the fire positions.

'Here, they lads has got shooters,' Wullie interpreted unsteadily.

Slowly we pivoted; very slowly indeed.

There were four of them, the first pair with the fire

power plus another two – obviously in charge – unarmed and wearing immaculately laundered white tropical rig; shorts, peaked uniform caps and the epaulettes of ship's officers. All watching us warily through Oriental and expressionless black eyes.

'You get in fligging boat . . . Quick time, no noise, hah.'

'Get the polis,' Wullie agitated nervously, probably for the first time in his misbegotten life. Trapp looked bleakly at him, then pointedly at me, and snarled, 'Don't be so *bloody* silly!'

I began to get even more angry than I already was. Scotsmen, Germans, Frenchmen, stateless men, Arabs . . . and now Chinese. Trapp attracted international trouble like a magnet. He was the human counterpart of the bloody U-bend in a lavatory – the part where all the dirt gets stuck. Desperately I stared around, then up at the high bows of the *Kamaran* in search for aid.

Then I breathed a sigh of relief. The troglodyte silhouette of Second Officer Spew lounged above us, gazing down from the rails with detached interest.

Ignoring the machinegun barrel which swung threateningly in line with my chest I began to wave frantically; appealingly.

Mister Spew gestured cheerily back with his one good arm – the one which hadn't been paralysed in a Marseilles brothel brawl, according to Trapp – and then turned conscientiously away to resume his cargo-handling duties.

Mind you, there was no doubt in my mind that he would have noticed the machineguns, and the threat to his captain. If it hadn't been for that eye. The one with the acid innit . . .

'Awwww, get in the fliggin' boat,' Trapp growled.

Resignedly.

I suppose the small ship on the other side of the fairway could have been more fairly described as a yacht, really. At least a yacht in the sense that it didn't appear to have any cargo-carrying capacity; nor would the Kaiser have considered he was letting the side down had he owned it. Apart from which the Westland Gazelle helicopter secured to the snowy-white deck was an accessory far in excess of any standard merchant ship's inventory.

The launch sheered alongside an accommodation ladder diamond-bright with new varnish and holystoned treads. Two immaculately turned-out Chinese seamen took our lines without a word as the grumble of the engine cut. Suddenly everything seemed very quiet, and somehow ominous.

The officer with the three gold rings jerked his head. 'You all get . . .'

'I know,' Trapp completed mildly; maybe a little too mildly. '. . . up the fliggin' ladder. Chop, chop.'

I started to say reasonably, 'Look, mister, I don't know what you want me for, but I've just paid myself off back there. I don't have anything more to do with either Trapp or the *Kama* . . .'

Then the foresight of a sub-machinegun raked agonizingly across the small of my back and, after I'd stopped writhing, I chop-chopped in raging but very mute frustration after my rather more diplomatically-acquiescent fellow kidnappers.

Mind you, it *was* my first time to be hi-jacked. Trapp and Gorbals Wullie were beginning to accept it as routine. In fact Trapp was so much at home in the role by then that he even managed to revert to his usual appraisal of other people's assets as we were gun-prodded forward.

'Cost a few bob, did this ship. See that paintwork, mister? Three coats o' best quality marine gloss wi'out no holidays when they wus layin' it on. An' them decks . . .? Grade "A" sanded Burma teak; none o' yer paper-thin rusty steel. Sixty 'Ong Kong dollars a cube that set the owners back, an' even then they'd've had to fiddle an export licence . . .'

But by that time we'd reached the entrance into the accommodation; and even Edward Trapp became strangely silent as we were urged across the polished brass coaming which led to a macabre and lunatic wonderland.

And to Mister Chang. The most wondrous eccentricity of them all.

I didn't believe it. Not at first.

We stood there, the three of us, gazing around in dumb incredulity as our escorts withdrew unnoticed. Oh, admittedly we made a somewhat unconventional trio ourselves – me under my six-day growth and dyed hair; Gorbals Wullie with that grease-stiff Glasgae razor bonnet and his skinny figure encased in a scrofulous, fifteenth-hand Harris tweed suit which defied every effort made by the Arabian sun to parboil him within it . . . and Trapp, of course – as sartorially disgusting as ever in baseball boots, a pair of trousers that could have come off a three-month-dead corpse, a yellow-stained and turtle-necked submariner's jersey that I vaguely remembered from the Second World War, all crowned by a verdigris-braided master's cap above which the partly-severed top gently bounced open and shut as he moved, like an opened tin of dog food.

Yet even then we didn't feel too out of place. The interior of that dream vessel's saloon was a fantasy world; a time machine leading to a celluloid past in which good guys and bad guys, and tough guys and sinister guys vied with one another's images to steal the pictures. A claustrophobic gallery of hard-eyed, jut-jawed Hollywood heavies gazing bleakly down at us from jumbo-sized frames reminiscent of an electric theatre of half a century ago.

Bogart; Gable; Raft; Flynn; Ameche; Karloff; Edward G. . . . ! I rubbed my eyes and stared fixedly ahead but there was no relief; no lessening of the visual impact. I felt myself cocooned, overwhelmed by a nausea of thirty-five milli-metre nostalgia.

For that was precisely the effect it had, the pile-carpeted belly of that super-modern ship. Of a giant and lavishly presented movie nightmare; a cinema *grand luxe*; a monument to tasteless décor modelled on all that was ostentatious and brassy and vulgar in the glorious hey-day of the cinematographic screen.

While under those eternally fixed and dead eyes sprawled all the other trappings of that gaudy yet magniloquent era – red-flocked wall coverings; jazzy imitation-crystal chandeliers; cascades of royal purple drapes; coils of chromed tubular hand-rails and ashtrays and stanchions; green plush tip-up seats and plaster half-nudes thrusting pink-tipped, wire-framed mammaries from arched and hand-painted torsos . . .

'. . . it's beautiful!' Trapp breathed in dewy-eyed veneration, oblivious now to whatever nameless threat hung over his future. 'I 'aven't never *been* aboard a more beautiful ship, I 'aven't.'

'Magic, Captin,' Wullie confirmed. 'All they gangsters; mah boyhood heroes an' that's a fact.'

And finally an organ began to play – a cinema organ, needless to say. And then we met Mister Chang . . .

I stared even harder. I was fully conscious of the fact that my reflexes were letting me down, but I couldn't do anything about it. I just . . . well . . . stared.

The curtains flanking the end of the saloon parted slowly, dramatically, as the organ rose to a crescendo. Then the lights dimmed slowly, and the spotlights came on to bathe the revealed stage in a blue-tinged haze vaguely reminiscent of Red Sweetwater's sordid atmosphere – or the B-movie film set of a Chicago speakeasy, Twenties style.

There were three men before us; two standing and one reclining languidly in a high-backed armchair. The two vertical members of the cast were Chinese, as was the third, but they were dressed entirely in black . . . Chicago hood-type black, with wide-shouldered, double-breasted suits, pencil-line moustaches and brim-low fedoras masking only slightly the coldness of their eyes.

'They got Thompson guns,' Wullie stammered nervously. 'Ah've studied them, ah have. Real Tommy guns like a' the mobs used tae rub each other oot wi'. Alla best gangsters like Capone an' Legs Diamond an' that . . .'

'Shut up!' Trapp suggested routinely, not taking his fascinated gaze from the man in the centre; the Man in the White Suit. Because, as seemed bizarrely appropriate in this celluloid environment, White Suit formed the positive image in stark contrast to the negatives flanking him. Where they were black, he was white; even his eyes appeared to have no density at all.

Then he spoke. But not in any Oriental dialect.

'You dirty rats,' he hissed. 'You dirty rats hear me good. One false move outa you schmoes an' I get the boys to blast you . . . OK?'

'Cagney,' Trapp whispered ecstatically. 'Pure Cagney, so 'e is.'

'Christ!' I muttered faintly, just before the voice from the stage came again, but altered this time; much more nasal, almost a drawl.

'OK, sweethearts. I gotta proposition for you guys, a real sweet-toothed proposition . . .'

'Bogart now.' Trapp wriggled in pure appreciation. ''Umphrey bloody Bogart to the life, mister.'

'Who's he goin' tae do next?' Wullie twittered, every bit as carried away as Trapp was. 'Who d'you reckon he's goin' tae do next then?'

'You, probably,' I snapped spitefully. 'This could well be your Saint Valentine's day, laddie.'

I gazed tightly around, searching for an exit sign – illuminated, of course – from this crazy ship crewed, apparently, not only by resident lunatics but also a couple of visitors; but there wasn't one. Then I looked around again, taking in the opulent furnishings while remembering the sheer quality of the vessel I was in, the enormous cost of building and running her, and began to wonder just who were the real idiots.

And why we were here at all; and what did the extrovert Oriental in the white suit want of us . . .

'Mad, o' course,' Trapp loftily pronounced with a

complete disdain for discretion. It was as if he'd been reading my mind, with the exclusion of his own part in the lunacy. 'All Chineemen is, mind you, but that one in partic'lar's as nutty as a heat-struck stoker.'

But the man in the chair didn't seem to hear. In fact when his voice came again it was even more of a contrast; this time it was soft, with the impeccable accent of an English public school.

'Rather good, what. Oh, permit me to introduce myself . . . my name is Chang. Mister Chang.'

''Ow d'you do,' Trapp retorted, not at all put out by the abrupt change of tack. 'I'm Trapp – Cap'n Trapp. An' this here's my chief officer, Mister . . . er . . . Cooper.'

'No, I'm not,' I snarled childishly.

'. . . an' the tatty Scotch feller, he's nuthin' special.'

'Can you dae Peter Lorry?' Wullie asked hopefully. 'He wis ma very favourite villain, so he wis.'

Mister Chang smiled tolerantly and 'did' Peter Lorre. Wullie and Trapp began to applaud unrestrainedly while I pinched myself to make certain I was awake, and that this really was happening. Then Mister Chang waved a deprecating hand and rather regretfully rose to his feet.

'Thank you, thank you, gentlemen. Your appreciation is more than gratifying . . . one of my little foibles, you understand? It truly is a pleasure to be able to share, all too infrequently, my passion for the great days of the silver screen with fellow moving-picture afficionados.'

I wondered sardonically whether or not he realized that Trapp and Gorbals Wullie would have shown equal, if not even greater enthusiasm for the type of moving-picture show exhibited above the bar at Red Sweetwater. But then Mister Chang altered course yet again, almost imperceptibly this time, and I sensed the crunch was coming.

'I believe you are doing business with an old acquaintance of mine, Captain Trapp. With a certain Mister . . . ah . . . Zarafiq.'

'Ah, now that would be tellin',' Trapp hedged virtuously. 'I don't discuss my business affairs with no one. It wouldn't be profeshnul ethics . . .'

Mister Chang gestured and one of the men in black stepped forward and took aim at Trapp's head. Trapp never even blinked an eyelid.

'. . . but on the other hand I b'lieve in the free exchange of ideas. In a nutshell, Mister Chang – yeah.'

Chang jerked his head dramatically. 'OK, Bugsy, park the rod. There ain't no need to blow the guy away in dis moment a time . . . Thank you, Captain; your frankness is most refreshing. Perhaps you would also confirm that your intentions regarding the forthcoming voyage of the *Kamaran* are a little less than . . . ah . . . honest? That my associate Zarafiq has, in fact, offered you the sum of twenty-five thousand pounds as an inducement to sink her after, shall we say, diverting her cargo?'

'You said he was only paying you ten thousand, Trapp,' I accused in bitter, if not entirely surprised reproach.

'You said he wis only payin' you five, Captin,' Gorbals Wullie supplemented in a squeal redolent of shattered illusions and faith undermined.

'I wus goin' to bank the rest for you, dammit,' Trapp muttered with only the slightest suggestion of questionable honesty. 'You'd jus' spend it all on food an' clothes an' that otherwise.'

But the look he threw at Mister Chang indicated that Mister Chang, just like Mister Zarafiq, had unwittingly placed his career in dire jeopardy. While, being Trapp, he didn't miss the opportunity of scoring at least one return point when it came to the question of revelations – or of establishing that Mister Chang's intelligence service was not the only efficient vehicle for gathering rumour.

'This yacht – it's called the *Illustrious Dragon*, ain't it? I noticed that much when we come alongside after we wus kidnapped.'

'Kidnapped, Captain Trapp?'

'Invited, Mister Chang. Yeah, well I heard about you too, then. Grockle the Fink wus talkin' about you one day. About you bein' one o' the Honk Kong number-one gangster boys . . .'

'Grockle the Fink is a purveyor of scurrilous rumour, sir,' the man on the stage corrected tightly, warningly. 'I am a businessman. Above moral reproach; an impeccable record in commerce.'

'Oh, aye? So all this wus paid for out o' the change the income tax man left you, I suppose . . .'

'Trapp,' I whispered agitatedly. 'F'r Christ's sake be a bit more diplomatic for once in your life . . . while you've still *got* a bloody life.'

But Trapp's mercurial temperament – like his avarice – tended to over-ride basic good sense.

'. . . can't stand yellow-men crooks what pretends they're bloody pure white lily ange . . .'

'TRAPP!'

There was a very long pause. I could plainly see the less-than-inscrutable rage in Mister Chang's rubicund features, and the way in which the black suits hopefully fondled their Thompson guns; then gradually the tension faded and Mister Chang picked an invisible thread from his virgin breast before he relaxed, and smiled.

'A proposition, Captain. A business proposition.'

'Oh, please yer bloody self,' Trapp muttered, still childishly piqued at the prospect of being forced into dispensing some more of Zarafiq's advance to Gorbals Wullie. Mind you, according to Trapp's standards, that money was more precious than life itself; the sharing of any part of it held much more horror for him than any threatened forty-five-calibre demise.

In fact, on reflection, Trapp would probably have agreed to sign a contract for his own suicide. As long as there was a profit in it.

'How would you like to earn an additional twenty-five thousand pounds, Captain? Plus, shall we say, a further ten thousand pounds as an advance bonus against your word?'

The silence this time lasted even longer. Only Trapp seemed unimpressed; unaware of the ripple of disbelief which stirred Gorbals Wullie and I.

'Oh aye,' he said placidly. 'And 'ow do I do that, mister?'

Mister Chang wriggled in self-congratulatory anticipation of his own genius.

'By offloading your cargo *before* you arrive at Mister Zarafiq's Gahmanian rendezvous, Captain; for delivery to certain Libyan acquaintances of mine instead . . . and finally scuttling the *Kamaran* as if by accident, in order to convince my dear friend Zarafiq that Allah can prove a most fickle and frustrating master.'

'But that's just what you're planning tae d . . .!' Wullie started to splutter before Trapp's elbow paralysed him from the neck down. Mind you, the upper part of him didn't need any treatment.

'You . . . you can't mean you wants me ter double-cross Mister Zarafiq, surely? An' then pretend the *Kamaran* sunk herself before she ever got near to unloadin' anythin' at all . . .' Trapp confirmed hesitantly.

Mister Chang smiled again. Delightedly. 'A jolly clever wheeze, what?'

'It . . . it's a master-stroke. It's a positiv'ly brilliant conception,' Edward Trapp breathed with the wide-eyed guile of an appreciative cherub. 'I gotter admit, Mister Chang – I couldn't never have thought of an idea as clever as that . . .'

'You know what you've done, don't you?' I snarled a little later. 'I mean, you do *know* what you've gone an' done, don't you, Trapp?'

He leaned phlegmatically over the *Kamaran*'s bridge front and calmly watched Second Officer Spew and Bosun Bligh moving around the foredeck; Spew checking, with what few parts of his anatomy still either existed or worked, that the hatch bars were locked, while the megalithic Bligh glowered and kicked at each lashing securing the deck cargo of bulldozers as though they were personal enemies.

'Wot've I done, then?'

I took a deep breath.

'You have, for starters, agreed to perpetrate one of the

most colossal insurance frauds in maritime history. Do you accept that?'

'Which one?'

'ZARAFIQ'S. ZARAFIQ'S BLOODY FIDDLE!'

'All right, all right,' he rejoined huffily. 'No need to get irritable.'

'And you have already told me,' I forced myself to continue in a lower key, 'that you've also sold that cargo to your own gangster pals just down the coast a bit, in Egypt. Right?'

'Well . . .'

'*Right?*'

'Yeah.'

I knew I was gripping the teak rail tightly enough to squeeze the sap out of it but I couldn't help myself. '. . . and now, in addition to all that, you have also committed yourself to delivering the same cargo that you've already sold twice . . . to a THIRD PARTY. To Mister Chang. In Libya.'

''E wus very persuasive,' Trapp argued doggedly. 'Thirty-five thousand quid's worth. Plus that mistake I made what gives you an' Wullie a bit extra; though it's wasted on 'im – he can't appreciate nothing properly unless it's stolen out've someone's hip pocket.'

'So who,' I persisted, firing each syllable with laborious clarity, 'do you intend to deliver to? Zarafiq in Gahman? Mister Chang's crowd in Libya? Or your own cut-throat oppos here in bloody Egypt?'

'My own, o' course,' Trapp said with a touch of virtuous asperity. 'I got principles, you know, mister. Apart from which, them partic'lar friends o' mine will use my liver f'r buzzard bait if I screws 'em.'

'Oh,' I retorted sarcastically. 'Oh, I didn't realize you mixed with nasty rough people like that. But, you see, there does appear to be one small difficulty arising from that decision of yours – just one tiny additional snag . . .'

I leaned over the rail and pointed with a shaking finger.

On the port side Fadel, flanked by the rest of Zarafiq's

Arabian heavy mob, still clustered with ominous watchfulness; drafted aboard to make absolutely certain that Trapp did deliver the goods to Mister Z.

'You may have convinced Fadel that you've been forced to sign on some pretty odd-ball characters as crew for the moment, Trapp. But has it ever occurred to you what's going to happen to that liver of yours when you do try to divert to your mates; when you finally do have to show your hand and double-cross both Zarafiq and Chang at the same time . . .?'

Because now, grouped on the starboard side and eyeing Zarafiq's already suspicious crowd with furtive hostility, there also huddled a quintet of Chinese hoodlums; each with the mandatory bulge under his pseudo-nautical seaman's rig, and all looking about as genuine in the shipboard environment of the *Kamaran* as chop suey at a bar mitzvah.

But lethal, nevertheless. Professional killers, every one.

'We're dead, Trapp. Whichever choice open to you is finally taken, the moment you do . . . we're all bloody dead!'

CHAPTER SEVEN

Of course it was too late for me to leave Trapp by then. The launch from Chang's *Illustrious Dragon* had kept a threatening watch on our gangway until the moment we finally sailed from Port Said. I'd even considered the prospect of going over the wall and swimming for it before we reached the end of the breakwater. But the launch had still been there astern of us; still watching . . .

. . . and now we'd been at sea for forty-eight hours. Yet still nobody had actually shot at anybody, while hardly anybody else had been slugged, mugged, knifed, heaved over the rails in the black of night, or otherwise generally discomfited.

Not that I felt any easier for the reprieve, mind you. Probably a number of kamikazi pilots had suffered much the same sense of false security, simply because nothing bad had happened to them during the first half of their flight – and even then their prospects must have appeared more hopeful than mine, seeing none of *them* had been tricked into carrying Trapp as observer.

The more I worried, the more my real employers' motives came into question. And how much they really knew about the true destination of the *Kamaran* – whichever that was. Obviously they were aware of Zarafiq and the Arab connection; but had they also known about Chang and his Chinese puzzle? And why, come to that, was the Royal Navy so concerned about what was, no matter how outrageous, simply a civil insurance fraud which didn't even involve a British vessel?

And why, come to that, were they convinced that a boatload of buckets and spades presented any kind of threat to Britain's national security? Even allowing for the fact that Trapp was in charge . . .

I'd called them last night for the first time; a hoarsely whispered entreaty with my cabin door firmly locked to prevent the imminent assault of an Arab gunman, an Oriental assassin or simply a common-or-garden Trapp-type thug.

'Charlie Tango Wun Fife, this is , . . er . . . Watchdog. Charlie Tango Wun Fife, this is Watchdog . . . Charlie Tango Wun, oh f'r Christ's sake, Charlie Tan . . .'

'This is Charlie Tango Wun Fife!' Charlie Tango Wun Fife had retorted, his disembodied tone displaying a firm hint of static-warped reproval. 'Request you observe correct voice procedure . . .'

I didn't know who Charlie Tango Wun Fife was, but I did describe *what* he was. I also passed on a few random comments regarding service voice procedures before I got down to the real, spy-type nitty gritty of reporting that the reason the *Kamaran* wasn't bound for Málaga, Spain, was because the Mister Zarafiq they already knew about had apparently bribed Trapp to offload somewhere else first. But Trapp wasn't actually heading there either, because a certain Mister Chang/Bogart/Cagney had paid more for us to take the bloody stuff to his particular reception centre . . . only Trapp wasn't goin' there either, dammit, because he also happened to be under pressure from some other trigger-happy band of Tuaregs to deliver the goods that *they'd* already paid him for . . .

There had been a long silence; and then Charlie Tango Wun Fife had said in a very strained voice, 'Wait one.'

So I'd waited one. Then two. Then three and a nerve-twanging four . . . until Charlie Tango Wun Fife came back across the ether and passed on a reply from what I gathered must have been his admiral.

It meant he had to break with service voice procedures himself, that time. Because I didn't think there were any phrases quite like that in any Royal Navy communications manual.

After stripping away the descriptive passages they

ordered me to do nothing yet. Simply to wait. And report.

To be strictly fair to the Royal Navy, it wasn't only them who managed to turn those initial two days of the passage into a nightmare for me. And it certainly wasn't the *Kamaran* herself – she was a good ship; a real seaman's pride even if a little old-fashioned.

No, it was more the fault of Trapp's crew. Because they were utterly bloody useless.

Take the meal times, for example. Despite the fact that such a cosmopolitan gathering should, under normal circumstances, have offered a challenge to any chef worth his salt shaker, the outcome smacked not so much of an international gourmet's convention as a gastronomic obstacle course.

For a start Bosun Bligh had volunteered to do the cooking. Or perhaps 'volunteered' wasn't quite the right expression in that Trapp had initially been forced to persuade the *Kamaran*'s chief petty officer a little – like pounding him continuously with a marlin spike until he agreed to co-operate.

Though to be fair to Trapp, this time it had all been the bosun's fault in the first place; why our original cook had suddenly found himself unable to continue with his culinary duties immediately after lunch on the first day.

As Trapp had remonstrated later, 'Yeah, well I knows Choker Bligh don't exac'ly like tomato soup, mister. But that weren't no real reason ter dip the poor bloody chef's 'ead innit, wus it?'

. . . and then there was the general atmosphere in the saloon; again hardly conducive to the sort of jollity and good fellowship one might reasonably have expected to aid one's gastric juices in their task even if Choker Bligh's productions had been digestible.

There were three tables running fore and aft, the two outboard ones being set for passengers and 'special advisory crew' – meaning Chinese who everybody, including Fadel, now recognized for what they were –

ocean-going yobbos. Which left the centre table reserved for what could be loosely described as the ship's 'officers'. But even that arrangement wasn't quite adequate; the way we'd placed all Zarafiq's clique to port and all Chang's gang to starboard in order to separate them. Because it still meant that one half of each mob were required to sit with their backs to their enemies on the other side of the saloon, if you see what I mean.

So the final seating plan agreed on was accomplished by every last hood from both factions perching grimly on the extreme outboard sides; all facing inwards towards each other, and all eating stolidly with one hand holding their forks while the other hand rested warily inside bulging lapels.

And all facing the centre table where I, not at all hungry whatever the quality of food, dined precisely in the middle of any impending cross-fire . . .

I gazed morosely around at my companions on that second day out. Trapp, as master, had taken his rightful place at the head of the officers' trough where, with typical disregard for the finer points of etiquette, he now lounged, baseball-booted feet comfortably propped across the table top and dog-tin cap flat aback on his head, awaiting the latest creation from *la cuisine de M'sieu Bligh*.

At the opposite end squelched Chief Engineer Maabud somethin' or other, dripping a steadily expanding film of oil on the carpet and fiddling nervously with what had been a serviette a few moments before but now looked more like a diesel-soaked ball of cotton waste. Nevertheless I felt grateful our ex-engine-driver chief was up for his meal first – the second engineer picked by Trapp was really dirty, the kind've company that would have made a sewer beetle want to take a shower. I did hope Maabud wouldn't succumb to his usual thing, though, and feel socially over-awed in such élite company, because that meant he'd be back down on the deck grovelling, and then Trapp would have to get up and irritably kick him back into his chair, and that would create even greater tension than there already was . . .

. . . and then there was Mister Spew.

It was very difficult to concentrate on eating when you were facing Mister Spew. I mean . . . well . . . so few parts of our grotesque second officer actually worked, while those bits that did only managed to move in articulated jerks which tended to spray the major part of any forkful in a sporadic arc long before it actually completed its voyage to his mouth. Quite often the game of culinary roulette wasn't ended even then, for Mister Spew's one good eye appeared to have difficulty in focusing properly, so as often as not whatever particles of sustenance which still remained clinging doggedly to his fork would miss his expectant maw anyway, to be propelled irretrievably over his left shoulder.

I did wonder for a while why he didn't simply scrape his dinner straight from the plate into his mouth. For one thing Spew, like Trapp, was hardly the type to feel hidebound by convention and, for another, such a minor breach of manners wouldn't even have been noticed in the saloon of the good ship *Kamaran*.

But then our reluctant chef stormed through from the galley on a tidal wave of blasphemy, dispensing grudging splodges of something unrecognizable from a grease-dripping plastic bucket . . . and I suddenly realized that maybe Dan'l Spew wasn't quite so bloody daft after all.

Later that night I saw Trapp climbing the bridge ladder towards me, followed by Fadel and a second Arab, and my heart sank. I knew the reprieve was over, and that eventually the shooting was bound to start.

Then the dim light from the binnacle fell across Trapp's features and my heart plummeted even further. He was wearing his clever expression, far too bloody clever by half, and that meant the shooting would probably begin even quicker because when Trapp got clever it meant he was even more intractable than usual. And conceited with it.

'Evenin', mister,' he called cheerfully.

I just glowered back and didn't reply.

He didn't reveal the slightest trace of shame. 'You never

been formally introduced, have yer? Well, this is Mister Fadel. Him an' his mate here 'ave come topsides to make sure we screws the insurance company on Zarafiq's behalf . . .'

The tall man with his arm in the sling moved impatiently, dangerously. 'Simply proceed with the course alteration, Captain. You have already been warned not to discuss Mister Zarafiq's business arrangements with your hired hands.'

I half opened my mouth to launch some withering broadside, but then became aware of the other Arab sidling around behind me and decided not to risk aggravating the situation even more. Trapp was perfectly capable of doing that without any help from me.

There was another factor to take into account; one which I'd already questioned, and that was the way in which Fadel continually fingered his injured arm while gazing so bleakly at Trapp. I had the unsettling conviction that they'd already met, long before the *Kamaran* ruined my life, and that the menacing Arab gunman had an old score to settle – intended to settle, dammit, whatever we did in the next few hours.

Not that you'd have guessed from the way Trapp was behaving.

'Bring 'er round to port then, mister,' he ordered imperiously. 'The new course is sou' west a half south.'

'What's that in proper language?' I snapped childishly. 'Most seamen stopped using compass points after the Armada ran aground.'

'Just do it,' Fadel advised flatly. He didn't need to add anything further; I could already sense the temperature dropping several degrees in that darkened wheelhouse, yet there wasn't even a gun in sight. Yet.

'Come port to two two zero,' I muttered tightly.

Gorbals Wullie began to spin the wheel and then stopped. 'Come tae . . . whit wis that?'

'That's the trouble wi' these hired hands,' Trapp couldn't resist observing to no one in particular. 'They don't know bugger all about nuthin'.'

'Come port to . . . oh, to south-west and a bloody half south,' I conceded. Wearily.

Trapp bumbled into the chartroom ten minutes later and grinned. 'They've gone below again, mate. Maybe it weren't such a bad idea, Chang insisting on puttin' his boys aboard as well. Now Fadel an' his bunch don't know whether to watch us or the Chinee mob the closest.'

I put on a surprised expression. 'Oh? But why should Fadel be worried? I thought you reckoned you'd been clever enough to convince him those Chinese were just ordinary, happy-go-lucky sailormen – despite the fact that they all eat in the saloon, as well as carry enough armament to start the third world war all on their own, of course.'

'Ahhhh, but Fadel don't think that at all. Because I very craftily let 'im see the Chineemen wus different . . . only he doesn't realize they're a part of another opportunist gang; he still thinks they're my own special boys, bodyguards sort of, which gives us a bit o' extra insurance without payin' no premium.'

'How do you know that? How do you know Fadel doesn't suspect you're intending to double-cross his boss in favour of Chang?'

'Because if 'e did then you, me an' Wullie woulda been floatin' astern wearing cement boots by now,' Trapp retorted, with a certain lack of diplomacy.

'But we wouldnae *float* wi' cement boots, Captin,' Wullie's perplexed voice drifted through from the wheelhouse.

'Shut up an' steer,' Trapp roared cheerfully. 'Anyway, mister, how could Fadel suspect a Chang take-over when I'm not even plannin' one? What's our course again?'

'Sou' west a half south,' I muttered, surrendering without a fight.

He looked at me with sly reproach. 'You mean two two zero degrees, don't yer? Proper seamen 'aven't used compass points since the Armada, mister.'

I closed my eyes, fighting the homicidal urge that threatened to overwhelm me, then opened them again and prodded the chart spitefully. 'That's where we're heading. It's called Africa, Trapp. The Independent State of Gahman to be more specific; sandwiched right in there between the borders of Libya and Egypt . . .'

'I know, I know all that.' Trapp finally wriggled with asperity. 'I'm not completely bloody ignorant. And we're not heading there much longer anyway, 'cause that's where Zarafiq expects us to deliver the cargo, an' where his bully-boy Fadel thinks we're goin' . . . until we gets there an' he discovers we ain't.'

I blinked. There were occasions when Trapp's conversation tended to become a little obscure, but I didn't need to consider his meaning too deeply; it had formed the basis for many sleepless hours over the past few days.

'Before you get us all killed,' I pleaded hopelessly for at least the fifteenth time, 'why don't you try and imagine precisely what Fadel and his gang are going to do to us when they do realize they aren't where you say we are?'

I got a certain gloomy satisfaction out of his confused expression that time, but it soon cleared and he looked all clever again.

'Ahhh, but by that time we'll be ready to offload the gear *there*, mister . . .'

His finger stubbed the chart at a desolate stretch of coastline – Egyptian, this time – between Bir Fuka and El Alamein. 'Which is where my contacts 'ave arranged to take delivery. An' once Yussuf MacKenzie an' his mad Tuaregs climb aboard, Fadel won't be given the chance ter say "Shalom".'

'Yussuf Mac*Kenz*ie?' I couldn't help blurting out.

''Is mother wus a Cairo belly dancer an' his father a Gordon Highlander.'

'Wan o' the cream,' the ever-eavesdropping Gorbals Wullie called from the wheelhouse. 'Braw lads, they Gordons. Bonnie fighters every wan. If they cannae find the enemy they get stuck intae each other, they boys . . .'

'Shut up,' prefixed Trapp before adding primly, 'Alter course to one five two degrees, quartermaster.'

'Eh?' the quartermaster echoed blankly from the other side of the bulkhead.

'Sou' east by a half east,' I translated furiously.

'Well how did ye no' say so, then?'

'Bloody ignorant Scotch savidge,' Trapp muttered.

The compass repeater over the chart table began to chatter as the ship's head altered away from Zarafiq's place of illicit business in Gahman until it steadied on Trapp's own rendezvous. Back in Egypt.

And I began to watch the door very jumpily. I had a feeling other people might notice as well, and get a bit annoyed.

'And what do we do if Fadel discovers the double-cross quicker than you think, Trapp? Like before we're under the protection of your pal MacKenzie?'

Trapp grinned in lofty derision. 'He won't. Them fellers isn't navigators like us, mister. Bloody ignorant Ayrab savidges.'

'Plus the fact that there's Chang to consider. Or had you forgotten that his representatives are aboard to ensure that you divert to his destination – which just happens to be in another country altogether, Trapp. In Libya.'

I ground to a halt as there was a movement at the door behind him but Trapp merely sniggered in outright scorn. 'The Chinees? Them heathens woul'n't know the difference if we wus ter steer 'em past Bucking'am Palace, they wouldn't. Bloody ignorant Oriental savidges.'

'Oh,' I echoed faintly. 'Then perhaps you'd better explain it to them.'

This time two Chinamen slid into the chartroom as Trapp swung anxiously. They were making no attempt to conceal the fact that they both carried guns, and both were eyeing the compass repeater pointedly.

'Quartermaster,' Trapp called without as much as a bat of an eyelid. 'Steer her a bit more accurate, dammit. Yer supposed to be on a course f'r . . . where is it, mister?'

'Libya?' I hazarded tentatively.

'That'll be . . . er . . . two three nine,' Trapp muttered, working desperately with the parallel rule.

I tried unavailingly to convert that to compass points for Wullie's benefit, but I wasn't fast enough.

'Sou' west by west a quarter west,' the foremost Chinaman translated with inscrutable expertise.

Which, apart from being a most remarkable feat for an ignorant Oriental savidge, neatly exploded yet another of Trapp's bigoted convictions. And also kicked the props from under his whole strategy of deceit.

Naturally it couldn't last. Trapp's master plan was collapsing in ruins; already he was fighting a losing navigational rearguard action. Every time the Chinese, or one of Fadel's Arabs, visited the bridge to check, the *Kamaran* was forced to alter course for either Zarafiq's Gahmanian destination, or Chang's Libyan rendezvous.

Each time they left the bridge Trapp would bring her back round until we were once again making painful progress towards his own offloading point in Egypt. And as he stared grimly astern at our tortured, corkscrewing wake, his mood got blacker and blacker.

Eventually I went below to my cabin. My only hope was that, if I left him up there, they would shoot him first. At least it would afford me one thrill of satisfaction before it was my turn. I even got a spiteful boost out of calling Charlie Tango Wun Fife for the second time. From now on anything I could do to screw Trapp just had to be a bonus, even if such a snide slice of self-gratification did promise to be posthumous.

Even that turned out to be as disappointing as it was vicarious. Any last-minute hopes I had cherished of the Royal Navy's intervention were dashed after I'd tried to explain to the bottom of my wardrobe that the *Kamaran* had now departed from her original Málaga course line for once and for all, and was now heading for Egypt.

Or Libya. Or the Independent Arab State of Gahman.

But North Africa, without a doubt. Oh, definitely North Africa.

For the moment . . .

Charlie Tango Wun Fife only acknowledged he'd received my pleading transmission with one word. It was a lurid but most unprocedural word, and simply established how uncouth some admirals of her Britannic Majesty's Navy could be.

Then I tried to get some sleep. But I couldn't even do that; there was no way I was going to manage that. Not with the knowledge that it was now past midnight; and that meant Second Officer Spew was keeping the watch.

For when Mister Spew was driving the ship lesser threats such as a bullet in the head held little terror. I discovered that fact the moment I eventually dragged my aching body above the level of the bridge ladder.

Just in time to see the street lamps of a whole bloody city bearing down on me at about twenty-five knots . . .

I'd actually been able to hear the music before I ever reached the bridge. It had appeared to be coming from somewhere over on our starboard side which meant that, as I was climbing the port ladder, all I could do was frown uneasily and wonder how an orchestra could possibly be playing some eighty miles off the North African coast in the middle of the night.

As the most obvious solution to the riddle sank in, so I began to run . . .

There was nobody up there, not on the port wing where I'd left Trapp ill-temperedly glowering astern a few hours earlier. I didn't hesitate to look for him; simply skidded in a frantic arc to make for the wheelhouse . . . and then stopped. Dead.

I could make out the hunched figure of Second Officer Spew lounging casually against the forward window ledge, Cyclopean gaze directed vaguely towards the bows somewhere. I could also see there was only an empty space behind the wheel where the helmsman *should* have been, which meant that we were either running on auto-pilot or, as seemed accepted practice on Trapp's commands, whoever should have been on watch had simply got fed up with steering and gone back to bed. I could also view – quite clearly through the side windows – the ever-advancing source of that nocturnal rhythm.

It was huge. No, it wasn't; it was bloody monstrous! A great, rearing blaze of light thundering directly towards us like a runaway maritime power station playing rock and roll . . . Rows of twinkling portholes; cascades of gaily sparkling fairy bulbs; even the strolling figures of jolly, fun-seeking voyagers clear as the scars on Mister Spew's face . . .

. . . I lunged for the wheel in terror, screaming, 'She's crossing from starboard to port, Spew. We're the *give-way ship,* f'r God's sake . . .!'

Slowly, almost wearily, the *Kamaran* came round as twenty thousand tons of rampaging accident roared across our bows like a berserk steamroller. I saw her own bow wave smashing into, rumbling clear across our fo'c'sle as we shied away; felt the whole ship leaning against the pull of the turn; glimpsed the rows of suddenly white faces gazing down at us from the steel cliff which kept on passing and passing, and still bloody passing . . .

. . . and then she was gone. Swallowed by the night as a fast receding glow and a fading reminder of how quickly death can take a sailorman even without the provocation offered by Trapp.

'That ship,' I eventually managed to whisper to the still-immobile and relaxed figure of our second officer. 'That was a twenty-thousand-ton cruise liner you nearly had us in collision with, mister.'

Only then did Second Officer Spew stir, and turn to fix me with his one good eye revealing a certain mystification.

'Yeah, Mister Cooper . . .' said Mister Spew blankly, but with a most earnest desire for enlightenment. '. . an' what ship wus that, then?'

'Five 'undred million Chineemen in the world,' Trapp

muttered petulantly a few minutes later, 'an' I has to get the one who can navigate!'

I didn't argue. There was no way you could argue with Trapp when it came to prejudice. Apart from which I was still having difficulty in speaking at all after Mister Spew's latest demonstration of how to sink yourself without really noticing.

'Which course is yous wantin' me tae steer now?' Gorbals Wullie called huffily from the wheelhouse. It had been my turn this time: to kick him all the way back to his place of duty from where I'd discovered him at the galley coffee pot, with a warning that if he ever left the wheel again without being formally relieved, then I personally would ensure he ate his own insanitary bloody hat – razor blades an' all.

'You got any o' them clever-dick Chineemen through there?' Trapp yelled nastily.

There was a moment of silence, then Wullie's voice came back. 'No! No, there's none o' they up here . . .'

'Then steer f'r Egypt, stupid. To MacKenzie's place like you already been told.'

'But, Captin . . .'

'Shut up!'

Trapp snatched for the log and began to scrawl the latest sequence of course alterations. By now there had been so many it looked like the journal of a wartime convoy steering a zigzag to confuse submarines. I wasn't too happy about the casual way he left it lying around, either.

'You know that log book alone is enough to earn us a throat cutting, don't you?' I growled bitterly. 'Anyone with half an idea of navigation could lay off precisely where we're really heading in two minutes flat.'

'An' you just heard Wullie,' Trapp countered irritably. 'There ain't no Chinees up here jus' now.'

'Fadel can't be all that far away. He'd have to be deaf, dumb and thick as Dan'l Spew not to have noticed when we tried to torpedo that liner back there.'

'Him?' Trapp jeered contemptuously. 'You think I'm bothered about the Ayrabs, mister? I told you before, they woul'n't know the difference between the Mediterranean an' a bucket o' water. They ain't civilized like you an' me, you know; they're jus' ignorant bloody . . .'

'. . . savages, Captain?' Fadel finished from the chartroom doorway.

'Well, I *tried* tae tell ye,' Wullie justified desperately from the other side of the bulkhead. 'And anyway, ye never asked me aboot Arabs, did ye?'

'Writing up your deck log, Captain Trapp?' Fadel asked with dangerous calm.

'Ohhhh shit,' I whispered. With hopeless fatalism.

'Jus' routine seamanship,' Trapp hurriedly dismissed the question, trying too late to shove the dog-eared book in the nearest drawer. 'Of course it's all scientific. Complicated like, unless you've 'ad speshul trainin' . . . wouldn't be of no use to someone like you . . .'

Fadel gently took the log from Trapp's hand as his companion placed a large revolver barrel beside Trapp's starboard ear. 'Oh, I don't know,' the Arab leader purred. 'I have dabbled a little in navigational theory myself from time to time.'

'When?' Trapp squeezed out almost pleadingly, while I became aware of a chilling premonition that yet another of Trapp's opinions was about to founder. Punctured, probably; by a ·45 bullet. 'When could an ignor . . . a gentleman such as yerself ever 'ave the chance to do somethin' as clever as navigashun?'

But diplomacy never had been Trapp's strong point. Not any more than humility, or the ability to keep up with a rapidly changing world.

'Could you bring yourself to believe they allowed me to do a little when I was sailing as chief officer aboard P & O passenger liners?' Fadel tendered, reaching for the dividers and the chart. 'In fact I spent some twenty-odd years as a deck officer in British ships before Mister Zarafiq was kind enough to offer me a more lucrative and enterprising position . . .'

'Ohhhh, shit!' I repeated, and began to watch the door

longingly for the first indication of the arrival of the reserves in the repellent forms of Gorbals Wullie and Second Officer Spew – as yet noticeable only by their absence.

Fadel didn't take very long, not even two minutes. Yet he was still smiling even as he turned back to face us, and suddenly his curious good humour all made spine-tingling sense.

'Now I really *can* kill you, Captain,' he said, and there was satisfaction in the bleak eyes. 'Mister Zarafiq promised I would be permitted to kill you eventually . . . in return for this.'

I watched his hand move downwards, caressing the crippled arm, and finally understood a little more clearly why he hated Trapp so much. Mind you most people did after they'd met him; if it hadn't been for the imminent curtailment of my own future I could easily have been on Fadel's side even then.

But Trapp quickly regained his own composure. In fact already he looked more outraged than apprehensive, more injured than guilty. 'You mean in the Channel that time?'

The scorn in his voice actually made Fadel blink doubtfully as he carried on, 'Christ, but I di'n't do no more than shoot you up a bit, did I? An' you still got one arm left, 'aven't you? So it's not like you wus as bad off as Spew who don't have hardly nothin' that works, is it . . . Anyway, Fadel, I resent your insinuashun˙ that I'm breaking my word with Mister Z; you ain't got one good reason to suggest I'd do a dishonest thing like that . . .'

I felt my own jaw drop, but it didn't matter. There was such conviction, such indignation in Trapp's outburst that even I was beginning to wonder who was misjudging whom. Suddenly it was Fadel on the defensive, angry and confused all at the same time.

'Your courses,' he snarled back, slamming his hand on the chart. 'They are like the wanderings of a camel from a poisoned water hole. To Gahman at first, yes . . . but then towards Libya. And then suddenly back to Egypt. And then Gahman once more . . . but then Libya again . . . and Gahman and Libya and *Egypt* . . .'

'You tellin' me I ain't able ter navigate . . .?' Trapp bellowed, the lid of his cap bouncing up and down in peevish indignation. 'You tellin' me I been steering the wrong courses jus' because you reckon twenty years onna P an' O boat qualifies yer to be a *proper* bloody sailorman, Fadel . . .?'

It was ridiculous, like some lunatic black comedy with each of them screaming epithets at each other while the second Arab stood uncertainly behind Trapp, still holding the gun underneath the violently bobbing headgear but unsure now of whether to shoot an' the hell with his leader's personal ambitions, or let Trapp explode anyway as his apoplexy passed safety point . . . or simply to retire to the wheelhouse to guard Spew and Gorbals Wullie – still apparently remaining discreetly under cover while the two main protagonists in this obscure navigational contretemps devastated each other with technical broadsides.

Then I saw his finger nervously toying with the trigger, and realized he was inclining towards the first and most practical option of all – to blow Trapp's stubborn skull clean off his shoulders – and felt sick with fear and unaccountably sad, all at the same time.

Not that Trapp appeared to bother even then.

'You taken magnetic an' not true courses f'r a start, you dry-land bloody Dervish. An' then you ain't allowed for deviation, 'ave yer? Nor variashun . . . an' wot about compensatin' f'r tides an' leeway an' that . . .'

Fadel's features were as suffused as Trapp's. He waved the brass dividers in a furious spiral. 'You take me for a fool, dung of a *fellahin* donkey? You consider me an apprentice on his first day at sea?'

'APPRENTICE!' Trapp boiled. 'I seen apprentices with more brains than you bein' sent for bucketfuls o' steam, dammit! I seen 'em twice as clever as you yet still daft enough ter go lookin' in the bosun's store f'r oil f'r the starboard lamp, Aladdin . . .'

'Kill him . . .!' Fadel spat in uncontrollable rage. 'Kill this spawn of a Cairo whore!'

Even as I gathered myself for a crazy, suicidal leap I knew it was too late, that I could never get there in time. Already the second Arab's finger was white on the trigger; the barrel of the gun behind Trapp's ear beginning to cock slightly, pulling upwards under the pressure of the coming death.

. . . until, without any warning, a very odd thing occurred.

When Trapp took all the steam out of the dispute by remarking, mildly and disarmingly, 'Hang on a minnit, lads. Well I never. Well, well, well, I'd never 'ave believed it . . .'

And abruptly the pressure on the trigger had eased unwittingly as the gunman leaned forward frowning, intently surveying the area of the chart where Trapp's grubby finger now indicated.

'Kill him!' Fadel snarled again. 'The pig attempted to divert me once before . . .'

'Oh, don't be so bloody intense,' Trapp reproved him with an even more disconcerting and good-humoured tolerance. Ever so casually he eased the dividers from Fadel's unwary grasp and tapped the chart with the points of them.

'Well, well,' he remarked again. 'Good grief. Well, well, well . . .'

Reversing the dividers he began to drum the table top pensively with the top hinge. Now the slender points were vertical, directed towards the deckhead above. He sniffed thoughtfully, raising his left hand to scratch his head; then he dropped that hand and fiddled a bit more with the dividers, tapping an absent rhythm as he scrutinized the chart minutely.

Then his head got itchy again and he began to raise his other hand, this time the one holding the dividers.

''Ere, you look at this then, Abdul . . .' he encouraged the second Arab in a most friendly and confidential way. Not that the position of the gun behind his ear varied in the slightest; the potential executioner's only reaction being to crane his head slightly further forward over Trapp's shoulder in a reflex attempt to see better.

And then it happened . . .

I was already diving for Fadel as he began to reach desperately for his own gun. 'Shoot quickly, FOOL . . .' he screamed as both he, and I, and maybe for one split second of horror, the second Arab too realized that Trapp's hand – still holding that shiny and so innocuous tool of the navigator's trade – wasn't going to stop to scratch his head at all . . .

. . . when its lazy, preoccupied rise abruptly accelerated to a vicious flashing arc which only completed its travel when the needle-sharp points entered the gunman's staring eye with hideous precision.

CHAPTER EIGHT

It wasn't simply the prospect of our immediate free-for-all which concerned me as I finally hurled myself towards Fadel. No, I'd long ago accepted that, when you associated with Trapp, you invited that sort of headlong rush into disaster as a matter of routine.

Only events never managed to end at that; in straight-forward homicidal chaos. Not when Trapp was involved. Somehow he had the uncanny knack of converting every simple, localized crisis into a full-scale bloody cataclysm which invariably embraced everyone else within pistol shot. He'd done that in the war – started off in a small way until his ideas got bigger and greedier, and eventually finished up taking on half Rommel's Afrika Korps as well as most of the German Navy because there was a chance of greater profit in it . . . but that was my other story; my other nightmare.

This was the present. While Trapp had just poked an Arab in the eye with a brass spear. And that Arab had a lot of very nasty friends . . .

I heard someone roaring in fright, '*Spew . . . WULLIE!* F'r God's sake help us . . .' as my shoulder hit Fadel low behind the knees. And then his Luger went off with an explosion which singed the back of my neck, and the terrified appeal got louder until I recognized my own voice . . .

. . . then my hysteria and Fadel's now unrestrained hatred and Trapp's bawling invective became over-whelmed by a steadily rising shriek as the second Arab skittered in demented circles on the deck, fluttering bloodied hands clawing at the glinting protrusion from his skull like a spitted, grounded butterfly.

'Spew . . . *WULLIEEEEE . . .*!'

96

The gun went off again, deafening in the confined space, just before I caught a fleeting image of Trapp staring, purple-faced and outraged, as his already appalling cap sailed through the air with a perfectly rounded and cindered bullet hole clean through the peak of it.

'That does it,' he screamed. 'That bloody does it then. Shootin' people's one thing, but gratituous dammige ter property's another soddin' ball game altergether . . .'

Then I saw his face, and knew that typical and black over-reaction to the irrelevant was merely a front; that Trapp's fury was generated by a passion much deeper, much more complex than a mere Luger round through his hat.

Still no Spew . . . still no Gorbals Wullie! Where the hell were they?

Trapp literally fell upon Fadel, fists and feet flailing in a blur of malevolence. The gun was still there though, still pumping shots automatically under the pressure of the Arab's startled clutch. The clock on the bulkhead disintegrated in a shower of tinkling fragments; the chart reared from the table as a furrow smashed a supersonic course from Sicily across to Mers el Kebir . . . the screeching horror of the skewered gunman rose a further octave when his kneecap blew away in a gory fuzz – and then mercifully and abruptly terminated altogether as the succeeding round took him neatly through the left temple.

The barrel swung wildly and laid itself directly at *me*. I lashed out in undisciplined panic and caught Fadel a glancing blow on his injured arm. He stumbled back in agony under the joint onslaught, stubbed his heel against the inert corpse of his associate, and finally went down like a felled tree.

But Trapp hadn't finished. I could only stare blankly in that following moment as he kicked viciously at Fadel's head then began to stamp brutally, maniacally on his fallen adversary's already mutilated limb. Then Fadel was screaming instead; writhing and retching and screaming . . .

T.P.—D

. . . I hauled Trapp away. 'TRAPP! F'r God's *sake*, Trapp, there's no need for more. No need to kill him too . . .'

Trapp glared at me murderously, yet there was a sort of vague contempt there too; I remembered over a quarter of a century ago when I'd watched that same look – the eyes of the other Edward Trapp, bitter and unforgiving – only they'd been directed over the sights of a heavy machinegun then, and laid on a lifeboat full of pleading women and children . . .

'But there is, mister,' he snarled with a cold venom which frightened me far more than any rage or passion. 'I 'ad three little Pakistanis once. On a boat in the English Channel. They wus my responsibility; my contract f'r delivery – yet that bastard cut their throats. Sliced their bloody windpipes jus' because they wus in the way, an' 'cause they 'ad a few gold trinkets . . .'

He booted Fadel, and Fadel screamed again. I picked up Fadel's Luger from the deck and pointed it at him tiredly.

'Do that again, Trapp, and I'll blow your fucking head off.'

A foreign voice shouted from a long way away, somewhere aft on the boat deck. Then another, and the clatter of running feet approaching, but Trapp didn't move for a moment.

Then he kicked Fadel once more; very deliberately. The Arab whimpered, and was sick, and finally retched into unconsciousness. Trapp smiled. It was a reckless, wolfish smile.

'Then you'd better pull that trigger quick, Number One,' he said mockingly, while listening to the fast closing sounds of danger. 'It seems like there's a few more wi' the same idea.'

I handed him the gun and walked through into the darkened wheelhouse without another word. I knew he was right, and that it could only be a matter of seconds before we both died anyway, very violently from either an Arab or a Chinese bullet. Even if the *Kamaran*'s crew did stand with us – and I doubted if any of them would – it still wouldn't save us now. From past experience Trapp had made bloody sure none of them owned any weapon more long range than a marline spike or a cut-throat razor, while all we possessed were the two surplus Arab pistols. Even then the Luger must be nearly empty.

Against a double squad of professional killers; one trio of whom would obliterate us as soon as they discovered their leader was *hors de combat* by the grace of Trapp, and the other group who wouldn't waste a lot of execution time either once they checked the *Kamaran*'s deck log against Mister Chang's pre-paid course instructions.

There was only one person in the wheelhouse – Gorbals Wullie. I could see his eyes following me like a hypnotized rabbit's from where he crouched behind the wheel. I could also make out the somnolent form of Mister Spew leaning in what appeared to be an excessively casual manner over the far side bridge front, staring down into the sea below, but I ignored him; my time promised to be a bit limited, but by God I was going to use it to full advantage.

Purposefully I started to move towards Wullie, hands out-stretched in anticipation. He seemed to shrink even more; wizened, ferrety features an apprehensive white blob in the darkness.

'Ah'm awfy glad tae see yous is all ri . . . er . . . Here, ah've been steerin' a braw course f'r you, Mister Miller, sir . . .'

'Come here, you gutless, dried-up little bastard, you,' I called wheedlingly. 'I'm gonna kill you, thistle head! I'm gonna tear your bloody arms out've their scrofulous sockets an' then I'm gonna beat you to death with 'em, you yellow-livered, spineless Scotch ferret . . .'

'But ah'm a tiger, sir,' Wullie protested weakly. 'You ask the captin – when ah gets ma dander up then ah'm a real tiger at the fisticuffs, honest tae God, sir. An' wi' the boots an' the razor . . . an' the heid an' the bottle an' the brass knucklies, so ah am . . .'

'You're nothing but a bagpipeful of wind. You are a cretinous, useless, conscienceless quitter. You could maybe have jumped Fadel back there; just taken him in the chartroom from behind – for Trapp's sake if not for mine, dammit. You must have heard me calling, only you were too bloody chicken-hearted to help, weren't you? And *that's* why I'm gonna punch the porridge out've you, sailor. Now!'

I drew my fist back enjoyably; there was just enough time left. The only problem seemed to be that Gorbals Wullie, terrified as he obviously was, still managed to produce a sly expression of injured outrage.

'And ah wis wantin' tae get stuck in, sir, ah swear it! Och but ma fists wis fair itchin' tae get tore intae they Arab lads an' save you and the captin, so they were. But ah couldn't, sir; ma sense o' duty an' . . . an' discipline, sir, just forced me tae stay here at ma post, sir. Just fightin' back ma true desires because of ma orders, sir.'

I held my fist in suspension and blinked. 'Orders? Whose orders, dammit?'

'Yours of course, Mister Miller, sir,' the frustrated tiger averred with the martyrdom of a truly misunderstood hero. 'Do ye no' remember what ye said ye'd dae to me if I ever left the wheel again wi'oot a proper relief?'

Then a Chinaman with a gun appeared at the starboard door; and an Arab with a gun appeared at the port door . . . and I gathered it was going to be largely academic as to who actually did kill Gorbals Wullie within the next ten seconds. Immediately after me.

Trapp. Now where the hell was *Trapp*?

Another four Chinamen arrived, and two more Arabs. We finally had a full house of heavies, all hesitating and peering through the unaccustomed darkness to discover where the trouble was, and who to shoot.

Only then did Trapp make his overdue appearance, framed in the light from the chartroom door; but again he'd altered disconcertingly. Now, in stark contrast to his earlier fury, he seemed confused and upset; a shipmaster driven to distraction by the perfidy of man.

'Oh my God . . .' he shouted hysterically. 'Ohhhh *God*

but they're hi-jackin' the ship. Stealin' my *cargo*, d'ye hear? It's piracy, lads . . . piracy on the high seas . . .'

I stared at him for yet another moment of incredulity, conscious of a strange disappointment – almost contempt – for the way his courage had finally deserted him. Until I remembered that the theatrical, distraught apparition was Trapp.

I began to dive for the deck, dragging a slower-on-the-uptake Gorbals Wullie in a dumbfounded heap beside me, just as the first Arab fired – straight through the wheelhouse and towards the only conceivable reasons for such an accusation.

Whereupon the startled Chinese instantly replied in kind, motivated by the equally certain assumption that Mister Chang's investment had finally become the target for the anticipated Middle Eastern counter-heist.

So naturally Zarafiq's men fired again. And then the Chinese. And the sole surviving Arab . . . and the last Chinaman . . .

And suddenly it seemed very quiet. Like being in a tomb, during a rest period.

Gingerly I sat up. Shards of broken glass tinkled to the deck as I felt myself for holes while taking in the details of bullet-riddled door frames blocked by similarly punctured and bloodied corpses, and the gaping glassless windows and the shot-scarred wheel. Behind me Trapp stirred too, lifting his head cautiously from where he'd nose-dived at the commencement of inter-gang hostilities; then he absently began kicking Gorbals Wullie out of what promised to be a permanently fear-induced state of catalepsy while, at the same time and to my intense satisfaction, looking uncharacteristically subdued.

'You've done it now,' I said firmly, uncompromisingly. 'Oh, you've gone far too bloody far this time, Trapp.'

There were shifty movements from the doorways as the *Kamaran*'s gallant complement gathered now that the shooting appeared to have ended. More and more of their dissipated faces hung suspended in the darkness until there was a sudden stir in the starboard press of ogling bystanders and Mister Spew shambled casually into the wheelhouse, matter-of-factly sidestepping the splayed Chinese cadavers and surveying the aftermath of Trapp's subtlety.

''Allo, 'allo,' Mister Spew greeted us, his one almost-good eye rotating in its socket like an interested ball-bearing. 'Did somethin' happen then? While I wus out doin' me duty on the bridge wing.'

I stared at him. While I thought I knew the answer I still had to ask. Just to make quite sure.

'Didn't you hear anything?' I managed eventually. 'Weren't you aware of anything occurring through here, less than fifteen feet away from you, that seemed just a tiny bit . . . well . . . odd? A little bit noisy?'

His eyebrows met in a ferocious vee as he creakily lifted his one good arm to scratch the back of his skull while trying painfully to think all the way back to four minutes ago. Then his expression cleared as he managed to remember.

'Ahhhhh, but I wus usin' me eye, then, Mister Cooper,' he pronounced with unshakeable logic. 'To watch f'r ships an' that, jus' like you said. And when I'm usin' me *eye*, then you can't possibly expect . . . well . . .'

'No,' I agreed. Because the worrying thing was that it didn't seem odd any more; almost natural somehow, aboard the *Kamaran*. 'No, Mister Spew, I suppose it would be most unreasonable of me to expect your *ears* to work as well. Not at the same time as you're using your eye . . .'

And then I went below to my cabin. And cried for the first time in thirty bloody years.

Trapp, of course, just had to follow me down some twenty minutes later. By that time I'd regained my composure, yet he still seemed uneasy, positively morbid in fact. That didn't prevent me from being spiteful, though.

'Well?' I snapped. 'How's Fadel since you tried to kick him to death?'

'Very quiet,' retorted Trapp, and sighed.

'It's a wonder,' I growled.

'Not really; not seein' Choker Bligh hit 'im over the head wi' a monkey wrench soon as he came round,' Trapp supplemented absently. Then he caught the expression on my face and added hurriedly, ''E's OK now! Choker's made him nice an' comfy down aft in the paint store. He's a tough desert bird, that Fadel.'

'What about the rest of the Arabs you shot?'

'It wus the Chineemen shot the Ayrabs,' Trapp corrected carefully. 'Or most of 'em, at least. Anyhow they're all dead as Tutankhamun except for Fadel.'

He saw me still eyeing him and added with a brief flash of self-righteous spirit, 'Well all I did wus to suggest the ship was bein' hi-jacked, didn't I? I mean I di'n't ackshully say to shoot at each other, did I? And I can't help it if them yo-yo's all jumped to the wrong conclusion, can I . . .?'

'And the Chinese,' I persisted wearily. 'All passed away too, I suppose?'

He wriggled uncomfortably and looked meek. Too bloody meek.

'I wus . . . ah . . . goin' to mention them. The Chineemen.'

'The Chinee – the Chinamen?'

'Yeah. The ones what got themselves shot . . . by the Ayrabs.'

I tried to stay calm. By God, but I did try very hard to stay calm.

'What about the Chinamen? Are you trying to tell me something I don't know, Trapp? About Mister Chang's Chinamen?'

'I jus' made a radio-telephone call. To Grockle the Fink back in Hong Kong. Cost a king's ransom, it did; all that talkin' at three, four dollars a minnit . . .'

'The Chinamen. NOW!'

Trapp glowered at me resentfully. 'Well how wus I supposed to know . . .? That Grockle, he said everybody knows about Chang an 'is boys, but I been outa the social whirl f'r a bit, 'aven't I? So how could I know them

Oriental chop sueys had a bit of an arrangement on the side; a bit on top of their respectable, day-ter-day villainy . . .?'

'WHAT *ABOUT* THE BLOODY CHINAMEN?'

'Well, Grockle says Chang's gotta contract with 'em,' he expanded hastily. 'To provide a sort o' part-time heavy mob f'r special delicate jobs – an' this was one of 'em.'

'Contract? Contract with who?'

'The CIA, o' course!' Trapp, suddenly impatient, stared at me in lofty disgust. 'Christ, but everybody knows *that*, mister . . . that Chang's boys aboard this ship was workin' for the United States Governmint. Before they got themselves shot, anyway – by Ayrabs.'

Trapp got peeved at my reaction eventually; glowering like a misunderstood child. But with him attack invariably afforded the best means of defence.

'All right, so what's Zarafiq up to, then? You tell me that, eh. I mean why's he involved with Chang an' the CIA? And if he is, then how does he hope ter get away wi' it – defraudin' the insurance companies? Jus' you tell me that, mister.'

'It's like declaring war,' I was still muttering dazedly, reflecting on how Trapp had disposed of what might have been five part-time CIA employees with one master stroke. '. . . Like declaring war on the United States of bloody America!'

'And why,' Trapp continued, pursuing his own deliberations with growing irritability, 'why are them CIA's so bloody interested in this ship anyway? And Chang, come to that. I could understand if he wus tryin' to pirate some other fixer's gear, but he ain't – *I'm* supposed to be doin' that for 'im – so if Grockle's right, which 'e always is, what's the real connection between Zarafiq, Chang an' them American secret services?'

It was my turn to shuffle guiltily, because I'd just remembered I wasn't exactly being square with him either; but that only made the riddle even more confusing for me – *I* knew the British Government were more than interested in the *Kamaran*'s future too. But why? Why go to all the trouble of infiltrating me aboard, simply for a cargo of bulldozers and picks and shovels?

'Why go to all this trouble,' Trapp deliberated morosely, telepathically, 'jus' for a cargo of bulldozers an' picks an' bloody shov . . .'

. . . and then we'd suddenly stared at each other for a long, long time. Before we began to run . . .

At three o'clock in the morning I stood beside Trapp on the *Kamaran*'s foredeck, and gazed silently into the now exposed depths of number three hold.

Gorbals Wullie was with us, and so were Second Officer Spew and Choker Bligh and a persistently oil-leaking Chief Engineer Maabud somethin' or other. All every bit as quiet and thoughtful.

And then, still without a word, we shambled in line ahead formation to scrutinize the contents of number two.

Followed by . . . number one hold. Right forward under the break of the fo'c'sle. We'd opened that up too.

With her engine stopped the *Kamaran* rolled uneasily, rather nervously, under the northerly swell while the cargo clusters at the crosstrees threw eerie, restless shadows which seemed to be reaching out for us; snatching at us with threatening, greedy talons. They gave plenty of light to pick out every detail of the huge and crouching bulldozers lashed along the well deck, yet even then we couldn't see what we'd been looking for. In fact there didn't appear to be another item of earthmoving plant aboard. Not a pick, not a shovel, not a pair of rubber boots. Not in any one of the twenty-odd packing cases we'd broken open so far.

Though there were other things, mind you. Lots of other things to stare at.

Like rows of grease-glittering Soviet Simonov Semi-automatic SKS Carbines; and quite a number of Kalashnikov PKS Heavy Machineguns; and piles of shiny little Czechoslovakian 7·62 mm pistols; and cases and cases of associated ammunition, as well as Polish anti-personnel grenades and East German manufactured land mines . . .

'Oh well,' I muttered eventually, consolingly. 'You may have sold the wrong stuff to your Tuareg pal; and signed your own slow death warrant on behalf of Mister Chang; as well as committing what is already, in the eyes of international law, piracy on the high seas. To say nothing of what amounts to declaring open hostilities against the United States of America . . . but at least Zarafiq can't accuse you of diverting his buckets and spades after this, Trapp. You most definitely aren't guilty of doing a silly, dangerous thing like that.'

He eyed me cautiously.

'No?'

I smiled tolerantly, shaking my head. 'Good Lord, no. Because, you see, all you've actually managed to do, old man, is to . . . well . . . to . . .'

And that was the moment when I began to shout. I couldn't help it, but I began to bawl at the top of my voice right there in the middle of the Mediterranean Sea. Loud enough for even Mister Spew to hear, and stare in one-eyed admiration all at the same time.

'. . . to steal the weapons of a whole fucking army, Trapp. An' that whole fuckin' army's gonna be FUCKIN' *FURIOUS* . . .!'

CHAPTER NINE

I used the concealed radio as soon as my fury had subsided to a burning resentment, and this time I didn't waste time talking to the hired hand; I demanded to speak directly to whoever the hell was running this goddamned lash-up . . . to Admiral Charlie Tango Wun Fife or whatever he called himself.

There was a tight-lipped silence across the ether, and then a gruff voice snapped, 'Watchdog – this is Charlie Tango Control. Pass your message.'

'News from the front,' I said coldly. 'Would you believe Mister Zarafiq's ploughshares appear to have turned themselves into very embarrassing swords?'

He didn't seem surprised. But then again neither was I that he wasn't – if you see what I mean. Because it simply confirmed what I was already finding out for myself; that there were a few minor omissions in the briefing they'd given me back in Hong Kong.

'Report your present course and speed, Watchdog.'

'I don't know and I don't care,' I retorted. 'I've resigned, Admiral. I'm not playing any more.'

The voice from the bottom of my wardrobe growled ominously, 'Say again, Watchdog?'

'You conned me into signing on with Naval Intelligence. You knew perfectly well that I wouldn't have been an outside runner for this bloody job if I'd suspected Trapp was even remotely involved; far less volunteering to sail as first mate with him aboard a crazy-ship full've pistol-packing Oriental G-Men and drop-outs from Al Fatah or whatever . . . Plus a crew of one-eyed hulks an' weirdos an' ocean-going freaks, currently sailing in ever-decreasing circles 'cause Captain Trapp up there's ungraciously coming to terms with the fact that he doesn't have a clue about what to do next . . .'

'Do?'

I halted for breath as Charlie Tango Control spoke precisely, commandingly. 'Then you must ensure that he continues his voyage. It is imperative that the *Kamaran*'s cargo should reach its original destination.'

'*Which* original destination?' I queried bitterly, forgetting temporarily that I'd already resigned.

'Zarafiq's. The *Kamaran* must reach Gahman at all costs . . . I say again, Watchdog – the *Kamaran* must offload her cargo at Zarafiq's original destination.'

'Oh, no.' I shook my head violently at the invisible admiral. 'We've got the hottest an' most lethal collection of armament aboard since the D-Day landings, yet I still don't know who they're consigned to; nor why the CIA are apparently working directly against the British Government . . . nor why Zarafiq ever trusted Trapp in the first place if his arms are so bloody important. Or why, come to that, your Royal Navy is so damn keen to ensure that communist-manufactured munitions are smuggled into what I always understood was a pro-Western Arab state . . .'

'Your Royal Navy too, Watchdog.' The admiral's tone had an edge to it now. 'I would remind you that you come under the Naval Discipline Act, and that the penalties for disobeying a command are most rigorous. Please remember that.'

'You haven't answered my questions again,' I snarled. 'You keep avoiding my bloody questions, mister . . .'

'This is an open radio transmission,' Charlie Tango Control boomed irately. 'You have already broken every security rule in the book, man. I cannot, and will not, communicate highly classified information by these insecure means . . .'

'SCREW your regulations!' I roared in fury, then, remembering where I was, dragged my voice down to a more discreet level of offensiveness. 'An' you can take your orders, Admiral, and stu . . .'

'Just do it, Watchdog. Just make certain that the *Kamaran*'s cargo reaches Gahman or, by God, I'll ensure that you never enter another British port or sail aboard another British ship again. There are no options in this assignment, which you willingly accepted – which means that even if you can't stand the heat, mister, you still stay in the blasted kitchen. Over . . . and out.'

And that was . . . well . . . that. I'd only learned one more thing; that if I didn't do precisely as I was told, then I might as well stay with Trapp and the rest of his maritime nomads until the inevitable occurred and they all either hanged, drowned or argued each other to death. I would be a pariah too. Stateless. A refugee from the Royal Naval Discipline Act.

I kicked the wardrobe a few times, then perversely began to feel better. At least I did have an objective, now; and as a heavily disguised Bert Cooper – who would miraculously disappear on the completion of this trip – had no retribution to fear from either Chang or Tuareg MacKenzie or even the CIA . . . All I had to do was gently to guide an already confused and uncertain Trapp's thinking along the Zarafiq course of righteousness and I would be free . . .

. . . until Trapp stormed in, with his face as black as thunder and a mood to match.

And growled savagely, 'I come to a decision, mister. It'll cost a bob or two in sacrifice, so 'elp me, but it's the only way ter keep us clear of all them vindictive bastids at the same time . . .

'. . . so you get Spew an' Bligh to swing them boats out, chop, chop. An' then come below to give me a hand – I'm settin' charges down there to blow this bucket clean out've the water. In just over an hour from now.'

I tried, but it was hopeless. Attempting to get Trapp to change his mind once it was made up was like asking a pyramid to move over to save steering your camel around it. Apart from which he was probably right on this particular occasion – if you considered his reasoning from an unprejudiced viewpoint, and didn't face the wrath of the Naval Discipline Act the moment the *Kamaran* slid beneath the waves.

I continued the argument right up to the minute when he showed me the first explosive in the cable locker – placed, I gathered, by Zarafiq's technical branch before she sailed from Port Said in preparation for a very expensive insurance bang. There were five more to activate – two in the engine room, two distributed along the shaft tunnel, and one right aft in the tiller flat; enough to scuttle her in seconds even in her originally anticipated and empty condition. Now, with a few thousand tons of cargo still remaining, she'd go down like a portion of Choker Bligh's plum duff.

'Look,' I persisted desperately, 'all you'll do if you sink her now is throw away the balance of the money Zarafiq owes you on completion. Why not deliver to Gahman first and then scuttle like your original contract stipulates?'

I could see his eyes misting at the thought of all that money being sacrificed, but he still shook his head fiercely. ''Cause if there's one bastard I hates more than Chang, it's that fairy Zarafiq, mister. An' no way am I goin' ter put a smile on either o' their faces by deliverin' what they must both need pretty bad . . .'

Then he hesitated, and there was a look on his face I hoped I would never see if his thoughts turned to me. 'Apart from which I'm goin' to kill Zarafiq. I made a sort o' promise, once . . . an' I can't part 'is cable if Chang or Taureg MacKenzie catches up wi' me first, see?'

And that was when I knew with a chilling certainty that Mister Zarafiq really was doomed. Which made him just like me.

'But Chang and MacKenzie will still be after you, dammit! Whatever you do they aren't going to get the cargo you promised . . . and the CIA won't be too fond of you either, now they seem to be involved.'

'They won't try an' find me all that hard. Not if they

thinks the *Kamaran* wus lost in a genuine accident . . . the Chinees is like that, with a funny sense o' fair play; while the Yanks won't risk no more publicity than necessary. Tuareg MacKenzie won't want no part of a cargo like that anyway – he's jus' a small-time operator when it comes ter arms an' stuff.'

'An accident?' I sneered, fast running out of logic. 'You call it an accident, Trapp. Blowing the bottom out've her with half a ton of plastic explosive.'

'Now you're nit-picking at technicalities – an' anyway, who's to tell 'em?' he asked cleverly.

'Fadel, f'r a start.'

'He won't be able to,' Trapp said, looking sad. 'The poor, helpless bastard's got hisself trapped in the paint store with no chance of gettin' to the boats.'

'No, he hasn't.'

'He bloody will have done. By the time the ship sinks.'

I didn't dare to argue any longer. That expression was back in his eyes, and there were times when even I had learned to bend before the vengeance of Trapp. Fadel was as good as dead anyway; as doomed as Mister Zarafiq – I wasn't aware of the precise story, even now, but I did know they'd both contracted their fatal illness some time ago, when the throats of three obscure Pakistanis were cut.

'Just get on with it,' Trapp growled, hauling a handful of pencil-shaped objects out of his pocket. 'These are the detonators they give me an' they're all I got . . . You own a watch, do you?'

I nodded peevishly; it was sheer luck that, so far, none of the crew had managed to steal it. Trapp began to unscrew the fusing mechanism in the casing with the ease of a man practised in the art of blowing things up.

'Good. Well this is a mechanical thingummyjig – once it's wound up we got exactly one hour afore it triggers that relay there . . . an' that makes the circuit from that battery there. An' then that little gilhicky flashes up the boiler, so ter speak . . .'

'All right, all right,' I muttered. 'What d'you want me to do?'

He clipped the first detonator into its housing and started to connect various wires, tongue sticking out in concentration. 'This'll take a while an' I don't want the bows ter start blowin' up while I'm still riggin' the after end. You wait 'ere; gimme ten minnits' head-start, and then wind up the timers quick as you can. One full turn clockwise, mister . . . then head f'r the boats.'

'No distress call? To make sure we're picked up? Which, incidentally, brings me to the small matter of how you're intending to persuade the authorities that the ship actually sank a long way north of here, seeing she should still be on a course line for Spain instead of Africa?'

'That's precisely why we ain't sending no mayday, mister. Because we sank yesterday, didn't we? So sudden there weren't even time ter get them poor Ayrab an' Chinee passengers off . . . which also accounts for the time it took for that northerly wind to set our boats south – like to this present position.'

'I still think you're making a mist . . .'

'Ten minnits,' he said pointedly. 'Or I'll send Dan'l Spew down to 'elp. An' he's more likely to set the bombs off there an' then, trying to make sure 'e does somethin' right f'r a change, seein' you keep on destroyin' his confidence like you do . . .'

He'd vanished before I could think up a suitable reply.

There was only me left now. Me, and the bomb.

I deliberately delayed a little longer than Trapp's specified ten minutes before I commenced my own task. I didn't want to catch up with him before he'd completed priming the devices. For one thing I knew that if I did – after having clambered awkwardly along the length of the ship's belly via the engineroom and the oil-slippery shaft tunnel – I'd have been more than tempted to have applied one additional clockwise revolution . . . to Trapp's stubborn bloody neck. While for another I'd finally made up my mind to . . .

. . . but then, just as I arrived at the last charge, the lights in the tiller flat went out as someone cut the main generator, forgetting, presumably, that it would tend to cease running anyway when the ship sank. I swore and fumbled for my torch, wishing Trapp might at least have waited for daylight, then gave a final vicious twist to the timing fuse and struggled up the vertical escape ladder to the poop.

It was almost as dark on deck, with the still-rising northerly wind clutching spitefully at my hair. Ahead of me I could see only the black silhouette of the superstructure scribing slow, rolling arcs against the stars while, somewhere, someone was shouting a string of unintelligible orders.

I frowned – Spew and Bligh had had over half an hour to lower the only two boats we carried; enough time to launch every lifeboat on a transatlantic passenger liner – so what the hell was all the noise about? Then I remembered that everybody screamed at everyone else as a matter of routine aboard Trapp's commands and tried unsuccessfully to shrug off the apprehension which touched me.

My unease didn't leave as I slid down the rails of the after well-deck ladder. It was an eerie sensation, being aboard a blacked-out vessel without even the comforting mutter of the main engine below your feet. Lonely somehow, as if I were the only human being left alive on the whole of the Mediterranean Sea despite that anonymous voice bellowing from forward.

But I wasn't. For one thing Fadel must still be aboard too, locked in the paint store and an unwitting candidate for a voyage to the bottom when the *Kamaran* finally did go down . . . I hesitated at the base of the ladder and swung to starboard, searching under the break of the poop towards the compartment where the Arab had been imprisoned.

And then I froze.

For now the steel door of the paint store was wide open –

and I didn't need a torch to tell me it would be uninhabited. Who could have released Fadel, and why? Certainly it wouldn't have been Trapp himself, because the vengeance of Trapp was an unrelenting force . . .

I began to run for my port boat station. There was nothing I could do regarding the disappearing Arab other than make damn sure I didn't meet him back there on that dark and threatening after deck, and Choker Bligh must be getting volubly impatient anyway, waiting to push the boat off as soon as I abandoned via the lower-deck boarding ladder.

I also began praying that they'd managed to get the boat's engine running; the prospect of the *Kamaran*'s crew trying to row conjured up visions of an epileptic water beetle attempting a getaway during a particularly unco-ordinated spasm. But even then every cloud had a miniscule silver lining – at least Trapp was the one stuck with Second Officer Spew as deputy commander of the starboard boat while I only had to tolerate Bosun Bligh as my number two. And I could always reason with Choker – as long as I got to the engine starting-handle first . . .

. . . then I'd reached the centrecastle deck, and looked over the side to where the lifeboat should be waiting. And stopped dead once again.

Because it wasn't. Waiting there below me in the water, I mean.

Oh, I admit I was far too hasty; far too quick to over-react by leaning out over the rail and hurling a string of imprecations across the dark sea like I did while all the time expecting Fadel to appear from the shadows and try to kill me. For this was the *Kamaran*.

Suddenly that anonymous shouting rose to a positive crescendo of rage, and I swung my torch upwards instead – beamed towards the boat deck – to discover that they hadn't even managed to swing the bloody boats out yet, never mind launch them and pull away from a ship that was expected to blow itself high as an overdosed junkie in about twenty minutes from now.

'Awwww *shit*!' I remarked to no one in particular.

And began to run for the ladder again.

We did get away eventually . . . after struggling dementedly with rust-bound blocks and paint-seized davits, and wasting a few more precious minutes pulling Choker Bligh's hands from around Gorbals Wullie's throat just because Wullie had suggested pointedly that a proper bosun woulda *seen* they things wis workin' when he knew there was due tae be a disaster . . . and inevitably sacrificing a few more vital seconds in disentangling Mister Spew from where he'd inexplicably managed to get himself trapped in the starboard lifeboat falls – plus a lot more time when, after smiling in amiable appreciation of his release, he promptly forgot he was on a ship at all, and shambled straight off the edge of the boat deck into the water fifty feet below . . .

They were still engaged in pumping our accident-prone second officer's bilges dry when Trapp finally managed to manoeuvre his frantically splashing boat alongside mine. We lay together about four cables off the darkened ship, and waited tensely for the *Kamaran* to have her accident.

''Ow long now?' Trapp called moodily.

'Four minutes,' I retorted with satisfaction. At least I could derive a certain bleak pleasure from the financial suffering he was enduring, apart from his natural aversion to sacrificing the only decent ship he'd ever commanded. Trapp was very much a seaman whatever his history, and even a pirate could shed a tear as he watched a prize slide beneath the waves for the last time.

A breaking crest came in under our stern and the boat wallowed into the pursuing trough to the accompaniment of Chief Engineer Maabud somethin' or other being seasick instead of trying to get our motor to fire. Then someone else joined in, and someone else, until we had a jolly chorus.

''Ow long now?'

'Three minutes . . . But more important, what happened to Fadel, Trapp? Who let him out?'

'No one did. He's still in the paint store – ain't he?'

'Not any more. The door was wide open when I passed.'

I could sense the growing anxiety in Trapp's growl. 'Well, 'e wus in there. All battened down an' waitin' to become a diver. I even sent Spew aft ter lock 'im in personally so's . . .'

There was silence. For a moment. Until . . .

'*Spew!*'

The sodden hulk of Mister Spew struggled to a sitting position. He still gurgled a bit, and squelched every time he moved, but some parts of him seemed to be working almost as good as new again. He might have got himself chipped about a little over the years but he was rapidly proving indestructible.

'Aye, Captin?'

'The Ayrab, mister . . . did yer lock 'im up like I said, did yer?'

'O' course I did!' Spew affirmed virtuously. '*And* I made sure 'e wus in there afore I did lock it, Captin. I ain't so daft I woul'n't check on a thing like that . . .'

'See?' Trapp bellowed triumphantly. 'Di'n't I tell yer I only employs the cream, mister? Good reliable boys the lot o' 'em.'

'Ho yus, 'e definitely wus in the paint store,' Mister Spew reiterated after laborious reflection. 'I saw 'im meself – when I give 'im the spare key . . .'

There was another silence; a slightly longer one this time. Before Trapp said in a funny voice, 'Why did yer give 'im the spare key, mister?'

'So's he wouldn't be stuck in there, Captin. When the ship went down.'

That perfectly rational explanation caused the longest silence of all.

''Ow long now?' Trapp muttered. Eventually.

'One minute.'

'Oh well,' Trapp commented philosophically. 'I suppose it won't make that much difference whether the Ayrab's sittin' onnit or innit when she blows. Not after she's converted ter bein' a submarine.'

And so we waited, two tiny boats full of seasick sailors, with the wind snapping the spray across our expectant eyes and the white-crested seas bearing down upon us from the north.

'Now!' Trapp muttered, oddly subdued. 'She'll be goin' any second now . . .'

But she didn't. For the pre-arranged time of the *Kamaran*'s violent death came, and passed. The silent black ship remained on the surface ahead of us, blatantly mocking us with her stability and comfort.

Two minutes went by. Then three. And then four, yet still nobody said a word. Until, five minutes after scuttling time, Trapp exploded instead.

'Them bombs,' he snarled furiously. 'Someone's scuttled me scuttlin' charges, dammit!'

'Well, I certainly set the time fuses like you wanted,' I defended myself truthfully. 'One full turn clockwise for each device.'

'I know yer did . . .' he roared back unthinkingly. Then added awkwardly, 'Yeah, well, I jus' thought I'd better check after you finished forward, di'n't I.'

'Obviously,' I retorted, with just the right amount of injured reproach. 'And thank you for your trust and confiden . . .'

'Christ!' someone squealed and I hurriedly swung to face forward again – neatly in time to see the rest of the *Kamaran*'s lights snap on with twinkling abruptness. Suddenly she was indestructibly alive again, all cheery and warm and illuminating the rows of green-tinged faces staring in astonishment.

'Who done that?' Trapp blurted in outraged perplexity. 'She's supposed ter be all blowed up by now. Who put them bloody lights on?'

'Fadel. It has to be Fadel . . .' I stood up in the boat and roared, 'Ship *oars*! Give way together . . .'

'Belay that!' Trapp began waving his arms in peevish temper. 'I gives the orders here, mister. I says where we go an' when we bloody goes. . .'

'Well, you'd better *give* 'em. We've got less than ten minutes to get back aboard, Trapp – Fadel's a seaman, remember? It won't take him longer than that to restart the main engine and switch her to bridge control . . .'

Stop panickin',' bawled a near-apoplectic Trapp. 'I won't have a chief officer what panics, d'you hear?'

'. . . and he's cold-blooded enough to run both these boats down before he finally disappears over the bloody horizon.'

'ROW!' Trapp bellowed. 'Row like you wus practisin' to be torpedoes, lads . . .'

And so we rowed; splashing and crab-wise, some even falling backwards off thwarts in a desperate, cursing attempt to regain the lee of the *Kamaran* before Fadel used her to kill us instead.

One hundred metres to go . . . seventy . . . fifty, with the great bulk of the ship now towering above us and the surging foam crashing and whirlpooling between the tips of her mercifully still static propeller. But then a sudden rumble and a cloud of black soot; the steady waterfall of coolant from her discharge . . .

'She's started up! Pull together, f'r God's sake . . .'

In the other boat Trapp began pummelling Gorbals Wullie in frustration. 'Row, stoopid! Don't jus' waggle yer oars like a spare whatsit at an orgy.'

'Stop that or ah'm tellin' ye this is the last time ah'm goin' tae travel tourist class,' Wullie shrieked back hysterically.

I craned forward, eyes frantically searching through the gloom while praying Fadel hadn't had time to haul the abandoned ladder back inboard . . . but no! There it was, just ahead now, with the painted white rungs gleaming softly from the overspill of the alleyway lights.

'Make for the falls,' I urged. 'Try to hook on to the falls, Bosun.'

'Go f'r the falls, lads,' Trapp was roaring simultaneously from the starboard boat. 'Get 'er alongside that ladder an' secure to the falls . . .'

'Way 'nough . . .' I screamed, suddenly visualizing what was about to happen. 'BACKWATEEEEER . . .'

The two boats came together with a splintering crash. Oars snapped like matchsticks, men cannoned into one another in flailing disarray, Mister Spew collapsed gigantically into the Mediterranean for the second time that night, and I became miserably aware of water rushing and gurgling through the shattered planking. Locked inextricably together like Roman war galleys we drifted and bumped along the *Kamaran*'s water-line until we finally came to the ladder.

Trapp clambered heavily on to it, gun in one hand and the expression of a man who'd already seen it all before on his face.

''E keeps on sinkin' my boats, that Fadel,' he snarled dangerously. 'I'm gettin' fed up to the teeth, the way 'e keeps on sinkin' my bloody boats.'

He began to climb in simmering fury, prodding an unenthusiastic and volubly protesting Gorbals Wullie ahead of him as the spearhead of the assault group. I watched Choker Bligh step on the ladder holding his sheath knife like a beloved friend, then called after them.

'I suppose I'd better hang on a bit and save Mister Spew first.'

Trapp's response was typically petty-minded.

'Oh, please yer bloody self,' he acknowledged indifferently. 'Even if yer does, the stupid bastard'll jus' fall in again . . .'

Of course they never caught Fadel. It was lucky for all of them the Arab had given priority to restarting the *Kamaran*'s engine and not to selecting a machinegun from her rather excessive stock . . . but there were a great many places for a man to hide, and I didn't think we'd see him again until he was ready. I could only hope that I could persuade Trapp not to cut off his nose to spite his face again and that maybe Fadel would leave us alone. His interests, in that way, coincided with those of mine and the British

Government – to allow the *Kamaran* to continue her interrupted voyage to Gahman.

If Trapp could be convinced. And if he didn't solve the problem by suffering an apoplectic stroke when he finally discovered *why* those scuttling charges hadn't gone off in the first place.

So it was with a little less than enthusiasm that I finally ran my captain to earth in the engineroom, engaged in what was, to my mind, a most ill-tempered and ill-advised examination of one of the errant devices.

Choker Bligh was kneeling with matching stupidity beside him while, at a more discreet distance, Gorbals Wullie and our chief engineer hovered like athletes keyed up for the starting pistol. Mind you, in fairness to Bligh, it did strike me later that they were unnecessarily tense – if the bloody thing did go off none of us would need to move a muscle to make it clear through the engineroom skylight forty feet above us.

'So there you are, mister,' Trapp greeted grumpily. 'An' where've you been then?'

'I told you; saving Spew for posterity.'

''Ardly worth the trouble. Where is 'e now?'

'Leaking seawater all over the bridge. He's on watch.'

'But we ain't goin' nowhere. The ship's stopped.'

'That,' I explained with enormous patience, 'is why Mister Spew *has* been put on watch. Once we're under way again I'd suggest we tie him up in his cabin.'

'Well, we won't be ever again – under way, I mean,' Trapp muttered grimly. 'Not once I finds out why these flamin' bombs didn't work, we won't.'

I didn't argue right away because that was the moment when Choker Bligh started prodding the dormant charge with his sheath knife. It didn't seem very scientific to me but I wasn't particularly anxious for them to discover the fault . . . and I certainly didn't want them to overcome it. Especially not while I was still in the engineroom.

Then Trapp turned his attentions to it as well and started to fiddle recklessly with the fuse setting, twisting and poking at it. The chief engineer immediately threw himself prostrate along the oily deck plates and began to pray hysterically while Gorbals Wullie stuck his fingers in his ears and screwed his eyes tight shut. Trapp ignored them.

'You sure you activated these like I told yer, mister?'

'I understood you'd checked them yourself,' I retorted pointedly. 'With one of your typical expressions of faith in your subordinates.'

'Mmmmm . . .' He began to unscrew the detonator housing while Choker Bligh inserted his sheath knife under the magnetic clamp and tried to lever the device away from the side plates.

'You'll break yer knife,' Trapp warned helpfully.

Choker Bligh broke his knife.

'F**@£*"&****!' said the bosun. Predictably.

'Stupid bastid,' commented an already disenchanted Gorbals Wullie. Suicidally.

Eventually we managed to prize Bligh's hands from around Wullie's scrawny throat for the second time, then Trapp went back to unscrewing the detonator. I moved over and said anxiously, 'Look, why can't you just forget the scuttling idea and deliver to Zaraf . . .'

He withdrew the housing and held it up. The pencil-shaped detonator had gone.

'Who's taken me detonator?' he asked blankly.

I swallowed and backed away, conscious, at the same time, of a rather odd scraping sound which appeared to come from the other side of the hull plates; from outboard the *Kamaran* itself. Right then I was more concerned with the purple flush rapidly spreading upwards from Trapp's collar, though.

'Who's stolen me bloody *detonator*?' he screamed in growing outrage.

'Never mind,' I consoled. 'You said you didn't have any more, so now you don't have to make a difficult decision. Now you *can't* scuttle her you've no need to fight your conscience or anything. Just deliver to Zaraf . . .'

'I'll *kill* 'im!'

He took a running kick at the bomb. Even Choker Bligh was on his way to the deck plates this time as it took off from the *Kamaran*'s side, ricocheted noisily off the auxiliary generator, clanged against the block of the main engine and disappeared into the bilges with a muffled splash.

'I'll kill that bloody clever-dick Ayrab!' he bellowed again.

I removed my hands from the back of my neck and uncurled from the foetal position I'd adopted when he kicked the bomb. I blinked at him – I'd never thought of that.

'Who – Fadel?' I asked tentatively.

'An' who else, mister? Who else woulda wanted to scuttle me scuttlin' charges then?'

There was yet another strange noise from outboard, almost as though something heavy was being dragged along the water-line, but again I ignored it. Fate had dealt me an opportunity I couldn't afford to miss and anyway, now I'd got over my biggest hurdle, I was beginning to enjoy myself in a vindictive sort of way.

'Well, he's won, whatever happens. You can't sink her now, so there's no alternative but to go to Gahman seeing you can't just leave her floating around the Mediterranean.'

'Whit about opening the seacocks?' Wullie suggested helpfully.

I took a deep and patient breath. 'Largely because ships don't *have* seacocks. It probably comes as news to you and Trapp, but most shipowners are rather more keen to design them to stay afloat in the first place . . .'

The bumping sound came again but Trapp was in full fury now. 'I'll set her on fire, dammit!'

'You can't do that either. She'll only burn down to the water-line. *And* give away the fact that you were well off course for Málaga before you torched her.'

'Then I'll arrange a . . . a collision.'

'You wouldn't need to,' I said cheerfully. 'Just leave Spew on the bridge for a couple of hours on his own an' we'll have one . . . but you still got the same problem –

wrong time, wrong place.'

'I'm gonna sink this fuckin' ship if I has to fill 'er with buckets o' bloody water!'

'. . . only you're gonna find yourself filled first, schmoe – wit lead,' a familiar voice called unexpectedly from above. 'OK, you dirty rats . . . Freeze!'

'Here, that wis clever,' Gorbals Wullie said admiringly. 'Ah didnae realize you could dae James Cagney good as yon, Captin.'

But Trapp didn't answer. In fact he'd gone very quiet all of a sudden, after swinging to stare bleakly up towards the head of the engineroom ladder.

'I still don't think he can,' I corrected nervously, eyes following Trapp's.

I suddenly understood what the earlier bumps had been, then. They were the sort of sounds one ship makes when coming alongside another. A ship like, say, the *Illustrious Dragon* of Mister Chang.

Choker Bligh had turned as well, to gaze at the previously unnoticed group above with an expression hovering between disbelief, truculence and outright derision. ''Oo called me a dirty rat, then?' he growled ominously. 'Which one o' them pansy, fancy-dress Chineemen called me a rat?'

I was rather more concerned with discovering precisely how they'd managed to get alongside without being detected – then remembered Mister Spew had been up there on watch, and stopped wondering. The bosun began to move forward resentfully.

'Easy, Choker; they're only film actin', so keep yer temper down,' Trapp warned tightly, warily, but our pugnacious shipmate continued to advance in simmering outrage.

'I *eats* Chineemen f'r breakfast,' he snarled. 'Especially poncy, makee-believe tough guys o' Chineemen . . .'

Gorbals Wullie perceptively dived for the deck for the second time. Maabud somethin' or other didn't need to; he still hadn't got to his feet following his initial prostration.

'Belay that, Bligh!' I roared, watching the guns. 'They aren't pretending any longer.'

'F**** and **** and **** you, mate!' the bosun bellowed back triumphantly, not even hurrying as he advanced step by step up the ladder in scowling retribution. I met Trapp eyeball to eyeball as we launched ourselves simultaneously for the lee of the auxiliary generator.

'You shouldn't've given 'im an order,' Trapp bawled reprovingly. 'You *knows* 'e gets awkward an' bloody-minded when you gives 'im an order.'

The racketing snarl of Thompson sub-machinegun fire confirmed he was right. It also told us that the film script had ended.

That now Mister Chang was playing the part for real.

CHAPTER TEN

And so the ludicrous finally did give way to murderous reality.

No longer was there the nightmarish feeling of being a bemused stage extra on the set of some particularly bad 'B' movie; for this wasn't the lavish interior of a megalomaniac's ocean-going kinema fantasy any more, this was the engineroom of a mystery ship called the *Kamaran*. And that contorted and rather surprised-looking cadaver at the bottom of the ladder wasn't a prop man's creation – it wasn't even the faintly ironic aftermath of a hoodlums' shoot-out as had taken place on the bridge earlier; it was the bullet-riddled body of one of our own shipmates.

Oh, Chang still wore that ridiculous white suit with the low-brimmed fedora, and was still theatrically flanked by his two crow-black professional killers with their anti-quated yet devastatingly lethal Chicago Pianos and their ever-so-chilling menace as they gun-prodded us up the ladders towards the *Kamaran*'s deck; but there was no Cinemascope vista to greet us as we stumbled out over the coaming dragging our fear-paralysed chief engineer between us – merely the grey winter dawn, and the metallic crouch of the bulldozers on either side which belied the true nature of the *Kamaran*'s evil cargo. And the sullen, apprehensive faces of Trapp's spineless and degenerate crew revealing a depth of human inadequacy impossible to portray on any silver screen.

While Mister Chang himself had changed, too. All his eccentric good humour had vanished. From the moment of Choker Bligh's execution he never 'did' Cagney again, not even for the gratification of his greatest fan, Gorbals Wullie. Nor did he render a Bogart or a Raft, or the slightest suspicion of an Edward G. . . . in fact he only gave one impression as we continued making our way to the bridge – of a very angry and vindictive Hong Kong gang boss.

All of which blew yet *another* of Trapp's loftily expounded generalities; that the Chinese sense of fair play differs in the slightest from anyone else's. Or did it? Because it had never really occurred to Trapp that whatever Chang proposed to do to him was more than justified by what he'd been attempting to do to Chang.

But that was different. Or so Edward Trapp would have claimed.

I confirmed the source of that scraping noise I'd heard, as I trudged my way along what promised to be my last walk topside. Outboard of us and secured fore and aft now lay the slimmer, more delicate hull of the streamlined *Illustrious Dragon*.

And I learned how she'd managed to get there undetected when we finally arrived on the bridge to find Mister Spew gazing in singular mystification down the hole in the end of a Chinese gun barrel.

'Where did 'e come from then?' Mister Spew asked huffily as we approached.

Nobody shot him so I ventured a reply, gesturing cautiously towards the fifteen-hundred-odd tons of steel next door.

'How about from there?' I suggested ingeniously. 'He – in fact, all of these Oriental gentlemen – may very well have come from that ship there, Mister Spew. The one you perhaps didn't . . . ah . . . notice. When she actually arrived.'

Mister Spew studied our neighbour with his usual frowning concentration, and then a tiny spark must have jolted his brain into momentary activity, and given him A Thought.

'Ahhhh, well that explains it, don't it?'

Even Mister Chang leaned forward curiously despite his annoyance, waiting for Mister Spew's revelation. 'Tell us,

Mister Spew,' I encouraged.

'Yeah, well, I wus ackshully keepin' watch out over the *port* side, wusn't I then, Mister Cooper? But that ship's alongside our *star*board side, ain't it? An' you coul'n't hardly expect a man ter keep watch on . . . on . . .'

'. . . on both sides all at the same time, Mister Spew?'

'Yus, Mister Cooper!'

I turned to face Mister Chang's Tommy guns. And sighed.

Mister Chang didn't want to hear Trapp's ingenious excuses. But Mister Chang was indeed a bitter man, shocked by the perfidy of his fellow business associate – which meant Trapp – and the fact that Trapp had managed to prove himself even more crooked than he, Chang, was. Therefore he, Chang, could see no alternative other than to terminate their business agreement in the most expeditious manner available.

'Cancel me contract?' Trapp ventured hopefully.

'Shoot you,' Mister Chang amended. Emphatically.

'But you can't,' Trapp argued desperately. 'If you still wants this cargo deliverin' to . . . where is it f'r you?'

'Libya.'

'Yeah, there . . . Well, how are you plannin' to sail this ship all that way if you kills off me an' my boys, eh? You ain't got enough seamen to crew two ships, have you? While all said an' done your crowd is only Chinee fellers . . . meanin' no disrespect, o' course,' he added hastily.

'None taken,' Mister Chang smoothly acknowledged. 'But while I appreciate the loyalty of your own chaps, Captain, I feel sure that some of them may well be prepared to consider temporary employment with me rather than join you at the bottom of the sea . . .'

It struck me rather cynically that every last one of Trapp's revolting gang of loyalists would fall over each other's knives to get at his throat if such a gesture offered reprieve; but then the chat became a little more personal as far as I was concerned when Chang continued.

'. . . therefore my intention is merely to execute yourself and your officers, Captain. And pray that my humble Chinese replacements can cope with the task.'

Chief Engineer Maabud somethin' or other issued a demented shriek and fell on the deck again, which was a pity seeing we'd only just managed to prop him up after the last bout of hysteria. Gorbals Wullie, on the other hand, began to ease gingerly past the Tommy gun at the head of the bridge ladder.

'Oh well, ye'll no' be wanting me then. Ah'm not an officer an' that's a fact . . .'

'Oh, yes you are,' Trapp snarled spitefully. 'I made you up ter actin' third mate when Choker Bligh got hisself paid off.'

'Congratulations on your promotion,' Mister Chang offered with dry finality. 'But now, gentlemen, I shall return to the *Illustrious Dragon*. You will appreciate that I prefer not to concern myself with the . . . ah . . . more mundane aspects of my profession.'

He straightened his suit fastidiously while I stared around. There could be no escape this time; three Chinese guns covered us in anticipation of the grand finale. Trapp was still trying, though, irritably gesturing towards the simultaneously elevated and condemned Gorbals Wullie.

'Jus' look at yer. I'll not 'ave my officers lookin' like they wus apprentice cleaners inna Bombay sewer. Put . . . yer . . . cap . . . on . . . straight!'

I read the meaningful look that passed between them and tensed, beginning to hope again. But only for a moment – until Mister Chang waved a hand languidly to one of his companions.

'Please be good enough to remove the third officer's head-gear, Chu Jun-min. You may well discover several razor blades sewn into the peak; a somewhat crude and unsophisticated form of defence originating, I believe, in certain lower echelons of Scottish society.'

'Bloody clever-dick Chinees . . .!' Trapp roared in

explosive frustration. Gorbals Wullie simply turned whiter than ever through a combination of fear, unaccustomed skull exposure and nationalistic affront. I stepped forward hurriedly, risking the guns in order to delay Chang's leaving.

'You referred to your "profession", Chang. Which one did you mean then – as a hoodlum, or a heavy for the CIA?'

He hesitated and I was relieved to see him smiling, not angry any more. 'Your intelligence appears to be very efficient, Mister Cooper. I suppose no harm can come of my telling you – I am acting in a dual role, both for my friends in the United States Government and for myself . . . as an international businessman, I must stress.'

'Then why prevent these arms going to Gahman? It's a pro-Western power, isn't it . . . so why should the US wish to deny them military aid, Chang? Even stuff as illicit as this obviously is.'

Mister Chang's smile held a hint of patronage. 'Because the *Kamaran*'s cargo was not bound for a government destination, my dear fellow. Quite the reverse, in fact, as they were intended for a reprehensibly Marxist-oriented group masquerading as the Gahman Liberation Front. To be utilized in displacing the present administration.'

That little bombshell made both Trapp and I stare at each other in mystification; but if he was taken aback, then I was doubly so, for I knew one more fact which only made the riddle even more obscure – because it raised the question of why the British Government should be so intent on not only frustrating what would appear to be a mutually-beneficial American operation, but also in actively supporting a communist take-over.

Trapp, however, was typically more fascinated with the financial structure of intrigue. 'So where does your profit come in, mister?' he growled sullenly.

This time Chang hugged himself with delight. 'Modesty must forbid me to suggest the word "brilliant", Captain, but I do happen to have contrived a marriage of both my dearest political and commercial interests in this particular matter . . . You see, I have already arranged to transfer, for a most satisfactory sum, the *Kamaran*'s cargo to a splendidly right-wing group of chaps known as The Friends Of Libya – and they intend to employ the arms to bring down Colonel Qaddhafi's deplorably pro-Soviet regime. I do so dislike people such as Qaddhafi; idealists dedicated to eliminating the profit motive.'

'Ah,' said Trapp appreciatively, 'then you an' me do have somethin' in common after all, Mister Chang.'

'Not a great deal,' Chang retorted blandly. 'For you will be dead in a few minutes' time, Captain Trapp. While I shall still be alive and making money.'

I could detect impatience beginning to overcome Chang's desire to emphasize his own star qualities, and racked my brain to further delay the inevitable. 'So Zarafiq's just a communist dogsbody, eh, Chang? Or does he have an ulterior motive, too?'

'Zarafiq?'

I blinked; Chang's expression really did appear to be one of genuine ignorance. 'The bloke who planned this crazy voyage in the first place . . . Trapp's original boss.'

'Partner,' Trapp corrected pompously.

'Shut *up*,' I rejoined, much to Gorbals Wullie's satisfaction.

Chang's frown cleared and he looked aggravatingly knowing. 'Of course, Mister Cooper – Zarafiq. Your discretion at this late hour brings you great credit, though naturally we are all aware of Mister Zarafiq's true identit . . . but no. It is very wrong of me to bore you with such repetitive and time-wasting trivia . . .!'

'But we ain't aware,' Trapp snarled. 'An' I'm in no bloody hurry.'

I elbowed him out of the way in a last attempt to prolong the conversation. 'All right. Then what reason could some other western power have for trying to topple the present Gahmanian Government, Chang? Say . . . well, say Britain, f'r instance?'

I saw Trapp's eyes dilate in suddenly aroused suspicion and, to divert him from attempting to kill me before the bloody Chinese, added hurriedly, '. . . hypothetically, of course.'

Mister Chang merely laughed in even greater appreciation of my humour before disappearing from sight below the level of the bridge.

'There! You see how well informed you are, Cooper? Don't we both appreciate what a delicately balanced commodity crude oil can be in the scales of power; what a catalyst it can provide for devious political manoeuvrings . . .?'

'But I'm *not* well informed,' I howled in frustration. 'That's the whole trouble, Chang – I don't know a bloody thing, dammit! Chang . . .? Come back, Chang!'

But the next time I saw him he had already crossed between our two ships and was making his leisurely way towards the bridge of the *Illustrious Dragon*; a tiny, dapper figure far below me. And I knew with a sinking heart that, when he finally reached it, I would never have enough time left to discover the reason for my own death. What part Gahman's crude oil industry was apparently to play in it. And even more teasingly – why Mister Chang hadn't recognized the name of Zarafiq at first, yet seemingly knew so much about the man himself . . .

We seemed to stand on that bleak and windswept bridge for a very long time, waiting for Mister Chang to direct the last scene – at least for Trapp and Gorbals Wullie, and Maabud and Spew and myself – of the *Kamaran* epic.

Numbly I stared astern, out over the boat deck where the seedily-dressed bit-part players shuffled uneasily under the watchful eyes of two more Chinese sub-machinegunners, and further out across the after well deck where the monstrous bulldozers still crouched in metallic contempt for our human fragility.

There was nothing on the horizon. No maritime equivalent of the US Cavalry approaching in the manner so dear to a real Hollywood script. In this story-line such an ending was not to be anticipated anyway. The Yanks weren't coming, not this time. They'd already got what they wanted through the devious manoeuvrings of Mister Chang; now our only hope would have lain in the low, grey silhouette of a British frigate speeding to our rescue . . . but that didn't make sense either. None of this outlandish, unmistakably-Trapp confusion did . . .

'What're we waitin' for then?' Mister Spew asked impatiently.

Nobody answered. There didn't seem a lot of point in it, because even Dan'l Spew would understand when it did happen.

Down below us Chang reached the *Illustrious Dragon*'s bridge and looked up, savouring every moment of this, his greatest production. Beside me Trapp tensed; even Gorbals Wullie stuck his jaw forward like a cornered rodent preparing for a last mad leap at his tormentors. Chang raised one arm dramatically, and there was a metallic rattle as cocking handles were yanked back on three machineguns . . .

The roar, when it came, was almost as petrifying as the anticipated crash of gunfire.

And I swung involuntarily – to see a blue haze cloud of exhaust scattering in the wind across the after deck as the biggest bulldozer of all detonated into thunderous life. And then began to move . . .

Actually everyone turned with the shock of it. The gunmen; every seaman huddling along the *Kamaran*'s boat deck; the crew of the exquisite craft alongside us; Mister Chang himself . . .

. . . or nearly everybody, anyway.

Trapp's granite fist took one of the Chicago-piano players square on the side of his head; the crunch of shattering bone echoing sickeningly even above the bulldozer's inexplicable growl. Simultaneously Gorbals Wullie lashed out with one frantic boot, missed the second black-suited Oriental altogether, shrieked, 'Och, Jeeze, help me, Mister Cooper, sirrrr . . .' and flung himself under cover behind the already inert body of our chief engineer – leaving me staring into the swinging barrel of a bloody Thompson gun.

I had no option. I grabbed for it; clung to it like a demented leech, yanking and at the same time twisting frantically to one side as bullets ripped a flail of teak splinters from the grubby deck. 'Gettim!' I screamed. 'Aw gettim f'r Christ's sake . . .'

Hysteria! Bedlam! The engine note of the giant earthmover rising to a crescendo of unleashed power. Maabud and Wullie's terrified howls only fractionally less pleading than my own . . . shouting from the *Illustrious Dragon*'s decks too, now, and the chatter of other small arms opening up. What the hell was happening back there . . . but who the hell cares?

'*Hold* 'im!' Trapp bellowed irresolutely, torn between the priorities of reinforcing my gibbering desperation or going for the third Chinese sailor, currently restricted in his field of fire by his own comrade.

'WHADDYATHINKI'M*TRYIN*'TODOOOOOO . . .?' I squealed maniacally.

The boom of the earthmover's exhaust a slamming echo from every bulkhead now; and the tormented clatter of gears engaging at high revs. An explosive snap. Then another . . . an' another, like . . . like steel shearing under stress. Or wire lashings parting. The kind used to secure deck cargo . . .

Trapp's arm suddenly hooked around the neck of my trigger-happy assailant. The black fedora skittered away as muscles bulged, the arm constricting effortlessly; a grubby-jersey-covered tourniquet under compression . . . the Thompson gun ceased firing as bulging eyes stared from a suffused black face . . .

The third sailor stepping back in panic now; going to pull the trigger an' the hell with his mate. I started to dive for him but I knew I didn't have a chance . . . yet there was

Spew still standing behind; still surveying the grunting, struggling press of bodies with amiable detachment . . .

'Spew! Do somethin', Spew, f'r . . .'

Further shots – a fusillade of confused gunfire; and more wires snapping . . . the clatter and screech of tracks fighting for grip on the steel after deck. Something incredible was happening back there and I was never going to find out what it was . . .

Until Mister Spew said obligingly, 'Aye, aye, Mister Cooper.'

Before he picked the third Chinese gunman clean off the bridge deck. And dropped him neatly over the side.

Nobody paid the slightest attention to Gorbals Wullie as he cautiously eased himself from under the cringing blob which was our senior engineer officer, took a sly glance around to confirm the heat was off, then bubbled excitedly, 'Here, did yous see me then? Did ah no' sort they poofy Chinese fellers oot, did ah no'? Jeeze, but there's nae disputin' ah'm pure tiger at heart. A reg'lar tiger o' a lad . . .'

Then he too caught sight of what was happening down aft.

And added, '. . . so ah am!' before lapsing into stupefied silence. Just like the rest of us . . .

The starboard bulldozer, yellow paint already scarred by a barrage of futile ricochets, was actually beginning to turn. Accompanied by a final firecracker parting of over-stressed lashings – and with one set of tracks grinding full astern, the other straining under forward throttle – the roaring machine was swinging in great sparking jerks to face outboard and slightly ahead; slamming into the steel bulwarks with a diesel snarl of fury, crushing and battering outrageously at the only structure restraining it from powering clean over the ship's side.

'Christ!' I yelled as I recognized the hunched silhouette of the driver, squeezed as low as possible into the armoured juggernaut's cockpit. 'It's the Arab . . . It's Fadel!'

Abruptly Trapp found his voice too. 'What's 'e doing?' he snarled in rising petulance. Then both he and I saw precisely what Zarafiq's first lieutenant was attempting – and Trapp was diving for the Tommy gun still clutched by the dead hoodlum.

'Leave Fadel alone!' I bawled.

'Don't tell *me*, mister! Tell them bloody Chinees . . .'

Trapp hit the trigger and the yammering racket drowned his words. A thick cloud of cordite smoke blew across the bridge – and the first of the two gunmen guarding the *Kamaran*'s terrified crew jetted across the boat deck in a tumbling cartwheel of arms and legs. Immediately the second Changster stopped firing at Fadel and whirled with the fear of death clamping his finger on the button. A wavering spray of automatic fire splintered davits, doors, ventilators, lockers . . . and suddenly there was an emptiness about the upper decks of the *Kamaran*; merely the tail end of a group of airborne sailormen leaping for cover – and a singularly unhappy Chinaman with an empty magazine.

Trapp fired again. With cold deliberation.

Just as the clamour of the berserk earthmover rose to a new high. There was renewed shouting and a pandemonium of gunfire from outboard; running feet and the *whoop, whoop, whoop* of the *Illustrious Dragon*'s siren . . . the threshing of propellers punctuated by the dull chunk of an urgently wielded axe.

Gorbals Wullie said in an awe-struck stammer, 'Would ye look at that, then.'

I started to run for the wing and leaned far out, staring down and astern all at the same time. Below me, on the bridge of the smaller ship, Mister Chang was doing much the same thing, and in much the same manner – transfixed, with nerveless hands clutching the rails before us . . .

The bulldozer had actually begun to mount the bulwarks now; tilting at a crazy angle, lying over towards me with one steadily revolving track almost straddling the crushed and twisted metal barrier. The other, still skidding and sparking and rattling monstrously, spun as Fadel gunned the engine to full screeching power.

'He's tryin' to get it over,' Trapp's spellbound mutter from beside me. 'That mad bloody Ayrab's actually tryin' to drive it clean off've the ship . . .'

'. . . on to Chang's,' I supplemented in horrified fascination. 'Jesus, but he's intending to drop it square on Chang's after deck.'

It had developed into a macabre race by now; Fadel's resolution against the frantic efforts of the *Illustrious Dragon*'s crew. Already her screws were churning ahead in a panic-initiated error, causing the slim length of her to sheer bar taut on the umbilical cords still securing her alongside the *Kamaran*. Two . . . no, three axe-wielding seamen chopping dementedly at her fore and aft springs; a fourth running pell-mell for the last stern rope restraining her after end . . . Chang screaming orders in staccato Chinese – no need for a script any more, not for this strictly off-the-cuff epic he found himself starring in. And more men tumbling on to her decks with hastily issued weapons, firing unavailingly upwards into the underside of the juggernaut appearing above them.

Then there was a *crack*. And another, with the fuzzed and severed tails of manila whipping clear through the fairleads.

'The Arab's no' goin' tae make it . . .' Wullie shrilled in disappointment. 'Bow rope's away! Backspring's awa . . . och, shit, but that's yon fore spring away an' a' . . .'

Abruptly released, the slender hull began to gather headway, water lashing and curling under the rounded counter. Almost simultaneously Fadel's roaring gargantua rocked, squealed a final rage of sparking tracks, and jolted forward and upwards to mount the sagging bulwarks in grating tumult.

'Her stern rope,' I heard myself howling feverishly. 'Her

stern rope's still holding her . . .'

But it wouldn't for long. The Chinese seaman with the axe was racing towards it, already preparing to strike – until there was a shattering racket from beside me . . . and the last hope for Mister Chang kept on going right past the bitts on suddenly spongy legs, cannoned sickeningly into the ensign staff on the *Dragon*'s taffrail, and cartwheeled over her after end.

Trapp looked at me over the sight of the Thompson gun. 'It ain't what a British seaman would do – use an axe,' he said straight-faced, and then he turned and looked down from the wing of our bridge. And smiled. Straight into the shocked and staring gaze of Mister Chang below.

It was a terrible, anticipatory smile . . .

The ahead strain came on the *Illustrious Dragon*'s still-secured stern line and she began, once more, to sheer uncontrollably into the side of the *Kamaran*. High above her the fifty-ton pendulum of Fadel's bright yellow bomb hesitated . . . swivelled a little and dipped its nose, curtseying almost as if in farewell . . .

. . . and then started to fall.

Fadel abandoned his seat with the same cold precision he'd applied to every other act of violence he'd ever committed, and right at the last possible moment.

I saw him haul himself out of his seat, clinging to the machine with one hand as the other dangled uselessly, a permanent legacy of Trapp's vindictiveness. Then calmly, almost contemptuously, he launched himself as the juggernaut tumbled from under.

Only one bullet caught him in mid-air; ironically one of the last despairing rounds fired from Chang's decks before the shooting stopped and the survival game began. Fadel jerked, spun, and smashed appallingly to the scarred and tortured deck – and then I dragged my eyes away to watch the end of the *Illustrious Dragon*.

The plummeting bulldozer struck her port bulwarks and

carved a vertical gash from deckline to keel, compacting and rending the thin shell plating like paper. Immediately the sea began to rush . . . no, literally to fall into the cavity created. For a shocked second we found ourselves staring into the shiny depths of her incised engineroom, down upon the transfixed image of a little, gaping man wearing a snowy boiler-suit – and then there was only the thunder of water, and the gouting foam between, and the shrieks of drowning sailors.

The *Illustrious Dragon* began to fall towards us, capsizing faster and faster to port with her foremast arc-ing violently and her ventilators blowing off under the pressure of displacing air. Crewmen clawed maniacally to climb an ever-canting deck as a lethal avalanche of heavy equipment started to tear free under the list. Drums, rafts still in their canisters, lockers, even her immaculate motor launch itself tumbled and bounced down, through and over them. Chang's Gazelle helicopter and several screaming seamen careered seawards in a scythe of bloodied, snapping rotor blades . . .

. . . the *Kamaran* shied away in terror, hung for a dazed moment, then began to roll back to starboard as the weight of her arms cargo overcame her obvious revulsion at the mutilation of a beautiful sister. The *Illustrious Dragon's* streamlined funnel impacted with our centrecastle rail in a screech of rending metal . . . her foremast crashed agonizingly into the break of our fo'c'sle . . . Mister Chang, now able only to cling in abject terror to the wheelhouse doorframe, turned his bewildered head – saw the slab-steel battering ram of the *Kamaran's* hull bearing inward and down upon him – and died in a long, smearing shriek of disbelief as I turned away and retched.

She went down on her side, with her lovely flared bows rearing towards the sky and our own scarred freighter rolling drunkenly on a suddenly very silent sea. Only a few flotsam scraps surfaced in the whirlpool of the *Illustrious Dragon's* going – half a dozen face-down corpses; an inverted motor launch; a magnificently varnished accommodation ladder; a flotilla of swirling, unidentifiable things . . .

. . . and a plaster female nude, bobbing and grimacing up at us like some monstrously gaudy mermaid. Oh, and a picture. Of James Cagney.

CHAPTER ELEVEN

As soon as we reached Fadel we realized it was hopeless. Whatever the riddles posed by the *Kamaran*'s cargo – and now even further complicated by the suddenly dead Mister Chang's frustrating part-disclosures – they would never reach solution through the bloodied and pain-taut lips of Zarafiq's henchman.

In fact they were to be compounded. Fadel was still fighting, and defeating us as we gazed grimly into eyes which, even though rabid fanaticism was swiftly giving way to the dull sheen of death, still watched us as vengefully as ever.

'Oil,' I said urgently. 'What did Chang mean about oil, Fadel? And how does the *Kamaran* fit in?'

He smiled. It was the same sort of smile Trapp had directed towards the capsizing *Illustrious Dragon* a few moments before, and it made me feel cold all over.

'The Chinaman was a fool. Like all imperialist gangsters he only believed what he wished to believe, Cooper . . .'

The pain hit him and he arched, feet skittering in his own blood. But the smile was still there, beneath the sweat. I knelt beside him and supported his head.

'Then you are a communist? Chang was right when he said the arms are bound for the Gahman Liberation crowd . . . for the Reds?'

And that was when I discovered he wasn't solving riddles; he was simply posing greater ones.

'Ask yourself, Cooper. Why did we go to such lengths to secure the services of Captain Trapp . . . the industrious and so predictable Captain Trapp?'

I blinked. Even Trapp looked momentarily disconcerted. 'Predictable' was probably at the top of the list of most unlikely adjectives to describe his particular attributes . . .

so what did Fadel mean? What the hell was he insinuating?

Then Trapp had to go and approach the delicate task of extracting information from a dying man with all his usual subtlety. 'You're gonna be dead as mutton inna minnit, Fadel – so where's me detonators? Jus' tell me where you hid the detonators f'r me scuttlin' charges, then?'

The defiant smile faded. 'Detonators?'

'The ones you took while we wus abandoned. To prevent me from sinkin' this bucket.'

Fadel's contempt didn't diminish, though he was clearly confused too. 'But why should I wish . . .'

He writhed again, and suddenly there was blood coming from the side of his mouth. '. . . you must *sink* the *Kamaran*, fools. My . . . our employer relies on your . . . your . . .'

The Arab's eyes closed while Trapp wiggled in thwarted rage. 'Is he sayin' he didn't neutralize them bombs, mister? An' what does 'e mean – I got to sink the bloody ship, eh . . . An' what's Zarafiq relyin' on? Relying on my *what*, dammit?'

'He's going,' I interjected hurriedly, bending with my mouth close to the dying Fadel's ear. 'Who is Zarafiq, Fadel? Who is Mister Zarafiq?'

He opened his eyes again, just for a moment. But there was only one expression left in them now. Only one quite unmistakable expression before more blood spewed from the slack mouth and the light in his eyes faded for ever.

'Zarafiq?' he asked.

As though he'd never, ever heard that name before.

This time I was so furious when I reached my cabin that I literally hurled the bundle of newspapers camouflaging the bottom of my wardrobe in a wide, fluttering snowstorm before lunging for the handset like I intended to strangle it.

'Get him!' I yelled uncaringly when Charlie Tango Wun Fife came on the air. 'Jus' get your boss an' never mind the procedure crap! DO you read me loud an' clear?'

'Control,' the metallic voice of my admiral snapped almost immediately. 'Make your report, Watchdog.'

So I did. Most succinctly. I told him all about the abortive scuttling attempt, and the boarding incident, and the way Fadel had died while killing Mister Chang . . . and the way in which a great many other men had died when the *Illustrious Dragon* had been run over by a rogue bulldozer.

And then I told him quite calmly, without rancour, precisely what he could do with political manoeuvring which murdered sailors; and with unethical pressures which allowed professional sadists like him to lean on simple-minded amateurs like me in the name of patriotism; and what he could consequently do with the Naval Discipline Act from this moment on . . .

'. . . because Trapp won't change, Admiral,' I assured him. 'I've known him and his pig-headed, bloody-minded determination for too long. He's going to sink this blasted ship one way or another; and it won't make a blind bit of difference whether you, the Yanks, the Soviets, or the whole lousy lot of you together try an' stop him . . . and you want to know something else, Admiral?'

The tone on the radio was bleak. 'Tell me, Watchdog.'

'I won't either,' I promised. 'In fact those detonators I removed all that time ago – when I was working for you? Under the Naval Discipline Act . . . ? Well, I'm just going to give them right back to Captain Edward Trapp, and tell him to go right ahead and cause the biggest bloody explosion in the whole bloody world . . . Sir!'

There was a long silence. I stayed there with my head stuck in the wardrobe and a reckless if slightly fixed grin of defiance on my face, relishing every second of his obvious discomfiture.

Until he said, rather jovially, 'Splendid, Watchdog . . . Your suggestion approved.'

The grin slowly slipped to one side. 'Say again?' I echoed almost pleadingly.

'I do say again, Watchdog – your orders have been changed. You are now instructed to ensure that the *Kamaran* is scuttled with all possible speed . . .'

The old familiar prickle came back again and I gripped

the handset nervously. 'Wait a minute. Suddenly you *do* want this ship sunk. And Fadel inexplicably wanted it sunk . . . and Trapp's determined it's gonna be sunk. So now, Admiral whoever-you-are, I would greatly appreciate it if you would very kindly inform me why it's *got to be bloody sunk, dammit!*'

. . . so he did. He told me, very clearly and without the slightest hesitation. And when he'd finished I could only stare at the handset and marvel at the depths to which politicians could sink as well as ships . . . and feel deliriously happy. Because at last the heat was off. I would be free the moment the *Kamaran* slid beneath the surface of the Mediterranean Sea.

Oh, it still didn't explain Fadel's last impassioned demand; there was still no apparent reason why he and Zarafiq should wish to frustrate their very own operation. For Fadel undoubtedly was a communist sympathizer, so why prevent arms finding their way into communist hands? But that didn't matter. Not to me. Not any more.

It only occurred to me after I'd signed off that I'd never cleared up that other niggling area of doubt – who, or what, was the mysterious Mister Zarafiq himself? And why had Chang been so vague when his name had been raised . . . and Fadel himself, come to that, who'd actually worked for the man?

But as I said, it didn't matter any more.

I even smiled a greeting when Trapp came in, which should have worried him for a start. But he was wearing his usual black frown and simply glanced suspiciously at the newspapers still littering the cabin.

'Just clearing out,' I said hurriedly. 'For when we abandon again and scuttle her. Properly this time, because I've found . . . er . . . well, I found the det . . .'

'Don't tell me, because it don't matter,' Trapp growled with implacable resolution. 'I been thinking, an' I've changed my mind, mister. I've gotter contract; an' a contract's a contract . . .'

His jaw set like a defiant bulldog's. '. . . so we ain't going to scuttle this ship, after all, see? We're deliverin' as requested. All the way to Gahman.'

'. . . it's the best way I can get even with Zarafiq, I tell yer,' Trapp insisted for the fiftieth time as he brought the *Kamaran*'s head round and pointed her towards Gahman. 'Deliver the stuff like I wus originally hired to do.'

'But that's the whole point,' I retorted wearily. 'You can't get even with a bloke by doing precisely what he asks you to do.'

'But it ain't, dammit! Accordin' to Fadel it's in Zarafiq's real interests to sink the bloody ship . . . so if I don't, then it screws 'im good an' proper. Right?'

'Fadel was dying . . . rambling. You can't take anything he said seriously.'

Trapp looked at me in a funny, unsettling way. 'So you're sayin' Fadel was looking at everythin' upside down, eh, mister?'

'Exactly. Dammit, Trapp, he didn't even let on when I asked him who Zarafiq was . . . pretended he didn't even know the name.'

I purposely didn't mention that Chang hadn't recognized it either. That was another problem.

Trapp's voice was meek. Too meek. 'True. So when 'e pretended to be surprised when I accused him of stealin' me detonators . . . you claim he wus really admittin' to having done so. Right?'

After I'd worked out what he meant I stared at him uncomfortably. A warning note was buzzing at the back of my mind; he'd cornered me, damn his clever eyes – because if I denied the possibility of Fadel's implication, then I was tacitly admitting that someone else had disarmed the charges . . . and somehow I didn't feel this was the most diplomatic moment to come clean on that score. Until I, in turn, was hit by a flash of inspiration.

'Of course he was. Which only proves my point, Trapp – Fadel did prevent you from scuttling the *Kamaran* back there. And that, without any shadow of doubt, underlines his intention of getting her to Gahman. Which, in its turn, means that the only way you can hit back at Zarafiq is to sink her, here and now.'

'No, it doesn't,' he argued somewhat obscurely. 'It only proves Fadel wanted the stuff to reach Gahman.'

'But he told us to sink her as well!' I yelled, pushed beyond all reasonable endurance. 'Half a bloody hour ago, Trapp. He said we had to sink her . . .'

I broke off in horror. I'd finally done it. I'd finally fallen into the Trapp trap of arguing against myself. His eyes glinted triumphantly, but he didn't dare push his luck too far.

'Mind you,' he added generously, 'just before that he also tried to sink Chang – an' save the *Kamaran*. But that could've been for a different reason altogether.'

'Like what?' I snapped, interested despite myself.

'Like because he is . . . was definit'ly a communist, was Fadel,' he continued perceptively. 'And while there must be some reason why he an' Zarafiq don't want their own Red mates in Gahman to get the goods, maybe Fadel was equally worried by the prospects of Chang offering a mob of rightists the wherewithal to give Soviet-backed Qaddhafi the bullet. Right?'

I didn't answer. For once Trapp might have come up with a logical thought.

'Anyway,' he continued doggedly, 'have you forgotten that other remark Fadel made – about askin' yourself why Zarafiq ever got me ter do this job in the first place? About his emphasizin' me bein' . . . what was it . . . predictable?'

'Hah!' I snorted derisively, but he didn't get annoyed for once.

'Exac'ly. I even admit I tends to blow with the wind at times; change me mind on odd occasions.'

'You, Trapp,' I said sincerely, 'have just made the understatement of the year. Being about as predictable as an oven-roasted hand-grenade.'

He smiled; a little tightly certainly, but he did smile. 'So allowin' f'r me slight fickleness, if you'd been Zarafiq an' you really did want a cargo deliverin' – would you have come half-way round the world just to get me to do it for you?'

I frowned. He'd certainly made his point. Had I been Zarafiq, then the one way I'd have been certain of losing my investment would have been to employ Trapp. Especially if I'd made sure that Trapp became my implacable enemy first – like by kidnapping him, maybe. And sinking his little fishing boat . . . and killing a few passengers who'd been his responsibility.

It didn't help me; my interests were apparently coincidental with the extraordinary plans of Mister Zarafiq, in wishing to see the last of the *Kamaran*. But the argument was over, and Trapp had made up his stubborn bloody mind.

For the next hour or two, anyway.

'So that's why we're takin' Zarafiq's cargo right to where 'e says he wants it, mister,' he grinned cleverly. 'But just in case I'm wrong – not that I ever am, mind – but just in case; then we're goin' to prepare a little insurance policy afore we arrive . . .'

I eyed him anxiously. I'd seen him like this before, and it made me very nervous indeed.

'Insurance?'

'Remember the *Charon*?' Trapp mused wistfully; dangerously. 'Remember 'ow we used to fight the war with the old *Charon* – Number One?'

CHAPTER TWELVE

According to Trapp arrangements had been made for a local craft to intercept us well offshore, and lead the *Kamaran* into the river where Zarafiq's people would be waiting to offload her.

It had seemed a sensible proposal at first – a glance at the chart showed it to be one of the most desolate and ill-marked waterways along the whole of the North African coast – and explained, at least in part, why we were apparently instructed to make the entry during daylight hours only. Though that somwhat indiscreet proposal did tend to aggravate my already active unease the more I thought about it, considering the illicit nature of the *Kamaran*'s cargo and the clandestine standing of its Marxist consignees.

But then I began to brood on the words of the dying Fadel; to ask myself again and again why a man such as Trapp *had* been so essential to Zarafiq's plan? Because any crooked ship-master could have been relied upon to bring the *Kamaran* this far – and theoretically we were to be piloted through the only real navigational hazards of the voyage. Weren't we?

Or did the enigmatic Mister Zarafiq have something a little different in store? Assuming Trapp *did* go strictly against form, and still turn up at that offshore rendezvous . . .

Anyway, it had been a seven-hour run into the meeting point. I'd spent six of them arguing with Trapp; the seventh had been utilized in making . . . well . . . preparations. Actually there had been a further task I'd made up my mind to carry out – like replacing the detonators in the charges and sinking the *Kamaran* anyway. But for obvious reasons that had to be a very private affair, and Trapp hadn't left me alone for long enough to go to the bloody toilet with discretion.

He even followed me down to my cabin, still vociferously demanding my unconditional approval and totally ignoring the fact that we were about to make our landfall at any moment. Mind you, that act of recklessness did hold out one small glimmer of hope for me; with Dan'l Spew keeping the watch there was a reasonable chance he wouldn't notice anything particular up ahead – and solve all my problems by running full tilt into bloody Africa.

Unfortunately Third Officer Gorbals Wullie was also topside, strutting the bridge like a bumptious mini-vulture, and he'd been told very earthily by his captain precisely what would happen to certain parts of his anatomy if he *didn't* see nuthin' an' report it when there *wus* somethin' ter be see'd. An' reported.

Or something?

'Well, you can't say we ain't ready f'r every possible contingency,' Trapp challenged me complacently, flopping on to my bunk and idly leafing through one of the newspapers still littering my cabin like confetti.

'Chang probably said much the same thing,' I retorted acidly, 'before he got himself torpedoed. By a bulldozer.'

'That weren't my fault,' Trapp defended himself primly.

'Oh, no. Not any more than the Second World War was Hitler's.'

'Yeah, well . . .'

He lapsed into sullen but welcome silence and glowered at the yellowing newsprint while I gloomily inspected the mirror, debating on whether to depart this mortal coil clean-shaven, or just stay a scruffy corpse to match the rest of the *Kamaran*'s crowd. Trapp's contingency plans for entering harbour smacked more of the Fleet's preparations before the Battle of Trafalgar – I'd developed the firm conviction he intended to get us all killed even if the commies were awaiting our arrival with a brass band and a camel-full of cash.

Suddenly Trapp jerked up and muttered, 'Christ!'

I ignored him pointedly; I simply wasn't in the mood for two-month-old news about how the world was going to hell – especially as I seemed scheduled to get there ahead of it. He wasn't going to be diverted, though. Just stuck the paper between me and the mirror and squinted uncomfortably.

It was an old copy of the *Malta Times* with a photograph of a suavely smiling Arab on the front. The caption read: *Middle East oil price deadlock. Gahman Minister flies to further talks.*

Trapp waggled the paper urgently, persistently. 'Know who he is, do you?'

I sighed and scanned the opening disinterestedly. 'Sheik Rabah Moinzadeh, millionaire oil minister for the Independent State of Gahman . . .'

'No, he's not,' Trapp blurted, then took a deep breath and added warily, 'He's . . . er . . . well, 'e's Zarafiq.'

'Your jokes usually manage to kill most of the audience,' I growled irritably. 'Please go away, Trapp. I'm very tired and I'd like to shave.'

'It's *Zarafiq*, I'm telling you,' he insisted. 'The bloke who hired me. Fadel's boss.'

I knew then he wasn't joking. I knew that much by the knot expanding in the pit of my stomach but I still argued, more as a plea than a statement. 'But you told me Zarafiq was just a fixer, dammit. A crooked businessman . . . while this Rabah whatsit's a heavy political animal; a government minister . . .'

Before the final stages of panic set in I desperately absorbed the next few lines. 'Yeah, look . . . pro-Western negotiator representing the Gahman Government at current OPEC talks. Apparently highly unpopular with the rest of the oil-producing countries, too – they're the only big exporters still blocking further price increases in crude . . .'

I suddenly broke off, staring unseeingly at the page. 'It did confirm one thing – that my admiral really had been telling the truth earlier, regarding why the British

Government had such a close interest in the *Kamaran* – it also made Zara . . . Moinzadeh? Aw the *hell* with it . . . Zarafiq's motives even more obscure than before. For why should a government minister, of all implausible people, have any connection at all with a plot to bring his own government down? A millionaire at that – involved with politically-dedicated millionaire-killers? Because Arab power struggles tended to prove violently fatal to the losers . . .

'Maybe the *Times* has made a mistake?' Trapp offered without a great deal of conviction.

'Negative,' I assured him – this time with a great deal of conviction. 'It's you who's made the mistake, Trapp. You an' your bent-as-a-corkscrew profiteering.'

'There's no call to cast aspersions on me commercial ethics,' he muttered weakly. 'Anyway, what difference does it make? Zarafiq's still Zara-bloody-fiq, whatever 'e calls himself on the side.'

'Difference?' I spluttered. 'Difference, you ask? Well, I'll tell you what difference it makes, shall I? It means, you've finally overstepped your mark. It means, you aren't even the target for petty CIA agents an' Chinese Mafia men any longer. Not now, mister. Because this article means you've bumbled your misbegotten way right into the big international league, Trapp . . . in the firing line between governments and super powers an' even the . . . the Shell bloody Oil Company, dammit!'

'Don't you yell at *me*, mate!' Trapp finally exploded, having run clean out of what was uncharacteristic humility anyway. 'Whatever Zarafiq's . . . Moinzadeh's . . . *Zarafiq's* bloody fancy government title is, he's still just a greedy Ayrab at the end o' the day. 'E's still jus' lookin' for a fast buck . . . an' you remember, mister clever dick – I'm still way ahead of 'im. I'm still dictating the action, savee? I'm the one what's goin' to spring all the surprises. *Right?*'

There was an abrupt knock on the door. Trapp flung it open furiously to reveal Gorbals Wullie standing there, looking decidedly uneasy.

'What d'yer WANT?' Trapp bellowed.

Wullie shuffled. 'Ah've come tae report – there's a ship comin' up on the starboard bow, Captin.'

Trapp swung triumphantly. 'See? Di'n't I tell yer then, mister? Thick as two short planks, that Zarafiq. Sent 'is pilot boat out to meet us like a turkey volunteerin' for Chris'mas . . .'

'Och, is *that* all it is?' Third Officer Wullie breathed with obvious relief. 'I thought that – what wi' all they guns an' missiles an' stuff – ah thought it wis maybe a Gahmanian warship . . .'

It was very ungracious of us, on reflection. The way he was left lying on the deck like that, all bruises and scuffmarks and bitter disillusionment. After we'd trampled straight over him, heading for the bridge . . .

Once again I felt I was reliving a nightmare; slipping irresistibly back into the time-dimmed past, with the restless stirring souls of ghosts over a quarter of a century dead suddenly awakening, and touching me with fearful memory.

Even the silhouette of the fast-approaching warship was much the same; still the evil, predatory shape reminiscent of the German *schnellbooten* or the VAS-boats of the World War Two Italian Fleet . . . And I was still there beside Trapp on a sullenly rolling bridge, watching, and waiting, and becoming more and more frightened as I'd done so many times before during the old *Charon*'s violent passage through the sewer of clandestine warfare.

Not even the location had altered all that much, for this was still the coast of North Africa; only there was no rumble of distant artillery as Rommel's *Afrika Korps* fell back under the assault of a long-dissolved Eighth Army; and there were no scurrying, terrified supply ships to provide an ill-defended prey for the *Charon*'s savage rape.

But there was no pride of country now either, nor patriotism to dull the sickness and the horror of before . . . and then I caught the look in Trapp's eyes, and remembered that there never had been, not for him, and realized that only I had changed. Everything else about me, about the world I existed in, hadn't moved forward one little, faltering step . . .

'You know what to do,' Trapp said calmly. 'Jus' get on wi' it.'

I blinked at him incredulously. 'Get on with what? The game's up, Trapp. That's a warship out there – flying the flag of a sovereign state; not some sophisticated maritime crook like Chang or Fadel. I told you earlier; you've got yourself involved with the national leagues now, Trapp, an' you don't do what you're proposing against a whole country.'

He didn't answer for a minute, just gazed out at the approaching craft with expressionless eyes. She was maybe two miles away and moving on a fast interception course. Through the binoculars she didn't look quite so old-fashioned any more; already I could make out the lines of a quick-firing turret gun on her foredeck and the even more unsettling suggestion of a missile-launcher aft. *Schnellbooten* and VAS-boats suddenly seemed almost friendly by comparison.

'You reckon they'll just smack our wrists and tell us not ter be naughty boys again, do yer?' he said eventually. And very mildly.

'No! We'll be arrested and charged with gun-running. We bloody well deserve to be, dammit! But there are diplomatic pressures . . .'

I think I knew, even as I spoke, that I was compounding a lie. I knew it as I stared aft at the grey, stateless faces nervously lining our scarred boat-deck rails . . . oh sure, maybe there would be diplomatic activity on my behalf – especially as now there could be no prospect of the *Kamaran*'s cargo ever reaching the communist forces, and the British Government would be very pleased with their extraordinary agent Miller. But there would be no hope at all for Trapp and Gorbals Wullie and Mister Spew and all those other international losers back there. The Gahmanians would throw them inside and forget them . . . but at least they'd still be alive, and still maybe able to con or bribe or slither a way to freedom. Especially knowing Trapp . . .

One and a half miles off. And still closing relentlessly.

''Ow many people do yer reckon knows about this rendezvous?' Trapp suddenly asked. His voice was still calm, almost conversational.

'Not many. Presumably it wasn't exactly advertised in the local press. Us and Zarafiq, obviously . . . a few of the top communists. Fadel . . .'

I broke off. There was yet another group who was aware of the arrangements – I'd told them myself. But the British weren't likely to have tipped off the Gahmanian authorities; apart from the fact that they assumed Trapp still intended to scuttle the *Kamaran*, they would hardly be anxious to admit they'd been interfering in the internal affairs of a friendly state. Especially when, for most of the time, they'd appeared to be trying to engineer its downfall.

'Well, the commies woul'n't have blown the gaff,' Trapp pointed out with undeniable logic. 'An' we certainly didn't . . . did we, mister?'

'No,' I said. Hurriedly.

'An' Fadel's dead as a shorted-out battery. So who else could've?'

One mile away. Sailors running to man the forward gun, while the missile-launcher aft was swinging, vectoring with space-age precision. White caps clearly visible on her flying bridge now, closed up to action stations.

'You mean Zarafiq himself . . . Oh, forget wild theories, Trapp. And forget what Fadel hinted; a dying man's raving. I still say you're crazy . . . I mean, why should he go to all this trouble – and then cut his own throat when he's virtually succeeded.'

'I dunno . . .' Trapp said thoughtfully, again scanning the approaching warship through his glasses. And then he handed them to me with a funny, mocking smile.

'. . . maybe you oughter ask him yourself, personally. Before he kills yer.'

'Stop engine.'

Mister Spew shuffled forward and grasped the telegraph, frowning in concentration as he tried to remember which way to swing it. Gorbals Wullie, relegated to the wheel again despite his recent elevation to officer status, looked piqued.

'How do I no' get tae do the technickle things?'

''Cause it's 'ighly scientific, see? An' too complex f'r a junior member o' the wardroom to 'andle.'

'Ah'm a third mate.'

'You're bloody stupid . . .'

I only heard their inconsequential bickering as though in a dream, not even really aware of the throb of the engine dying beneath me as the *Kamaran* coasted slowly to a halt. The figures on the warship bridge filled my binoculars now; all dark-skinned and clad in service whites . . . all except one. The grey-haired man in the tweed overcoat who clutched his hat unsteadily against the forty-knot wind of their approach.

I'd only seen a photograph of him until now. On the front page of the *Malta Times* . . .

'Now do yer believe me, mister . . . about Zarafiq?' Trapp prodded from behind.

Half a mile to go and even the missile-launcher was trained on us now.

'I don't see what difference it makes. She's still a Gahman warship; and I'm still damned if I'm prepared to go along with your sort of action against the flag of a Western power simply to avoid arrest . . .'

Trapp was smiling all the time, only there wasn't any humour in it by now. Just a savage, wolfish mockery – and that terrible hatred.

'If you wus Zarafiq – or maybe I should say if you wus a certain Sheik Rabah Moinzadeh, who just happened to have the authority o' a government minister; maybe even 'ad a few sympathetic mates wearin' admiral's stripes. An' you'd been fixin' – for whatever reason you like to pick – to stab your own government in the back by supplyin' arms to the communists . . . An' you knew there were only a few blokes on a certain ship what could blow the gaff on you – what would you do to them, mister? If you had 'em under a gun? With a good excuse to make yourself a national hero at the same time?'

I began to walk away from him. I only turned back when I'd reached the head of the ladder leading to the boat deck and the life-raft stowages.

'I hope you rot in hell, Trapp!' I said as levelly as I could.

He allowed his smile to broaden to a fully-fledged grin. 'You'll be able ter make sure I do, mister. 'Cause we'll all be there together; all alongside each other . . . only you'll still be wearin' that uniform, won't you?'

I blinked at him uncertainly. 'Uniform?'

'In a manner o' speaking. The one you never took off all them years ago, not even after the old *Charon* was sunk. The one you wus still wearin' when I met up wi' you again at Red Sweetwater, mister. The one you've been wearin' ever since you come aboard the *Kamaran* . . . the Queen's uniform, Lieutenant Miller – the uniform o' the Royal Navee.'

And then he leaned out over the rail, leaving me staring after him like a stranded fish.

And roared, just like he'd done so often before, when so many other men had died. 'Panic party awayyyyy . . . *abandonnnnn ship!'*

CHAPTER THIRTEEN

It was the very first time I'd seen anybody doing anything right since I'd joined the *Kamaran*.

As a panic party they were superb. The moment Trapp gave the order our boat deck became a scene of ultimate hysteria. Life-rafts tumbled haphazardly from every stowage to land in undisciplined chaos on the sea alongside; release lanyards were tugged with undisguised anxiety; great yellow and orange balloons unfurled and inflated with irresistible snorts, shoving and bumping like water-lilies manoeuvring at the start of a race . . . apart from the rafts that never actually reached the water – those which blew themselves up while still on deck, scattering seamen and jamming alleyways just because some stupid bastard had yanked the lanyard before he jettisoned the gear . . .

. . . and then the actual abandoning. Men spurred into feats of athleticism by the closing menace of that quick-firing foredeck gun, sliding and gabbling down anything that offered a safe passage off the ship . . . ropes, ladders, snaking white fire-hoses; kicking and struggling to get there first; shoving each other away from – or over, come to that – the bloody rails in a multi-lingual frenzy of fear. And the triumph which transcended anything we'd been able to produce on the old *Charon* . . . the super-star of the *Kamaran*'s epic evacuation – Maabud whatsit, Chief Engineer, Egyptian State Railways retired.

He was magnificent. Still looking like an ambulatory blob of engine oil, he managed to fight his way right to the head of the queue for leaving. Then he changed his mind about going over the rail at all . . . and someone behind started kicking him and yelling for a knife or a spanner or jus' a fuckin' table leg ter smash 'is effin' 'ead in . . . so Maabud shrieked a descending prayer to Allah, reinforced by a shotgun spray of appeals to the mercy of Jesus, the compassion of Buddha, the infinite clemency of Shinto, Baal, Nekhebt, Xochiquetzal, Amen-ra and – just in case – Beelzebub an' a few assorted demons, all the way down to the Plimsoll line . . . and then changed his mind about the whole bloody idea and tried frantically to shin back *up* the rope again despite the flood-tide of survival-bent bodies pouring across his like lemmings on a suicide trip.

'Lovely boys,' Trapp said, watching with enormous satisfaction. 'If that don't convince them Ayrab matelots we're abandonin' f'r real, then I'm a gorilla's uncle.'

'How did you discover,' I muttered cautiously, lying flat alongside him under cover of the bridge wing, 'that I'm still working for the RN?'

In view of the probable outcome of the impending action it seemed a bit academic whether he was angry or not, but I was glad to register only a comparatively inoffensive conceit in the glance he directed towards me.

'I didn't. Not until I saw the look in yer eyes when I needled yer. But you always wus too honest, wusn't you?'

'But you must have had some cause, some reason for suspicion?'

'Just little things. The Sweetwater set-up – too pat by half, after I'd thought about it a bit. An' then there wus the fact that you kept on changin' your mind about whether I should scuttle this bucket or not – an' apart from meself, there's only one crowd can be so bloody awkward an' erratic.'

'Who?'

'The Royal Navy, mister. When they're tryin' to do the impossible an' steer a course dictated by the British Government.'

For a few moments I felt truly humble; quite ashamed, in fact, and grateful for the manner in which he accepted my admitted disloyalty. 'I'm sorry, Trapp,' I ventured, hardly able to meet his eye. 'If I'd known you were involved from the start, I'd never have agreed to do it.'

He rolled over, looked straight at me – and began to leer

again. It was that old, deprecating, utterly infuriating expression he always managed to produce when he thought he'd got me cornered.

'Apology accepted, mate. I always knew there'd come a time when you finally has ter admit I've always been right an' you've always been wrong. That you always does the daft thing like a bull at a gate, while I employs me superior brain an' me natural commercial judgement an' me subtlety . . .'

I sat up so suddenly I nearly forgot there was a ready-use missile-launcher and a hotted-up Oerlikon behind the thin wooden screen. But he'd done it now. He'd gone an' done it again, just like he always bloody would.

'Subtlety?' I yelled, without the slightest suspicion of humility left. 'You've got all the subtlety of a rogue Panzer division, Trapp. And I wasn't meaning it as an apology, anyway – I meant I wouldn't have agreed to the Navy's proposal if they'd told me you were involved, for one reason an' f'r one reason only . . . because I'd hoped I'd never ever bloody see you again!'

His ever-blossoming grin was as wide as the gulf between us. Yet it still couldn't quite mask the relief which seemed so incongruous under the circumstances.

Until he chortled, 'Lord, but you 'ad me worried for a minnit then. I could've sworn you wasn't never goin' to give me a good argymint ever again, the way you looked so bloody repentant . . . Now shut up an' keep yer head down, jus' like you done in the war – Number One.'

Twenty minutes later. Twenty everlasting minutes later, and that grey interceptor was still hovering a frustratingly cautious distance off our starboard quarter.

It had been very quiet on board since the crew had gone. Oh, there was still the faint vibration of the slowly-turning main engine as it idled on *stand-by*, and the sigh of wind-strummed halyards above the bridge and the sporadic clatter of an empty beer can discarded in a scupper, but nothing really to indicate there was any human life left within this tension-fraught circle of sea other than the subdued mutter of frightened men in the life-rafts bobbing alongside, and the more distant growl of the Gahman Navy craft's exhausts . . . and the thunder of my own heart-beats as the waiting continued.

Surreptitiously I glanced across at Trapp; yeah, he still looked the same as he'd done all those years before, with flint-hard eyes peering through the hastily formed slot in the bridge wing and that grim piratical determination a carbon copy of our previous war.

Our tactics were identical, too. Disconcert our enemy; lead him to believe the target was abandoned, the crew demoralized – which shouldn't be too difficult, not with Trapp's current band of shambolic anti-heroes – until he dropped his guard, came that little, unsuspecting shade too close, and then . . .

Only it wasn't as simple as that. Not this time. Because there was one major difference – for the *Charon*, despite her mouldering decrepitude, had still sailed to battle as a highly specialized coffin. She had been a proper Q-ship, with concealed armament and drop-down side plates and even a basic fire-control system operated from her bridge. She'd worn her apparent nervousness as a shield, and her false colours had been a major weapon in the strategy of surprise.

But this was the *Kamaran*; and she carried no surprise. The Gahman Navy knew precisely what she was, while Zarafiq knew Trapp's history perhaps a little too well to allow him to live long enough to strike . . . apart from the fact that we had virtually no camouflaged fire positions at instant readiness, and no Bofors gun or 4·7-inch havoc to release at the command of a specialist rating's finger.

We had no specialist ratings, come to that – only Gorbals Wullie crouching on the boat deck with a bravado fuelled more by terror than true Scottish grit; plus three vaguely Greek seamen cowering behind the deckhousing without a weapon between them simply because they'd been too bloody paralysed with fright to abandon ship in the first place – and Second Officer Spew, who was the one man I didn't want on board, and who'd already ambled out of sight a few minutes ago carrying a grey-painted box he'd discovered somewhere, despite my frantically hissed plea to jus' lie down an' go to sleep.

Staunch, bumble-headed, screw-everythin'-up-proper Mister Spew . . .

'They're comin',' Trapp suddenly offered with enormous satisfaction. 'Di'n't I say they'd come closer, then?'

I wriggled over beside him and squinted through the peep-hole. The trickle of water under the uneasily cruising Gahmanian's bow had risen to a distinct flare as she turned towards us. A flash from her bridge betrayed binoculars inspecting – searching – the life-rafts in which most of the occupants now cringed, hidden from view by the automatically-inflated canopies.

'Stay outa sight, boys,' Trapp urged unnecessarily. 'Keep under them awnings like I told yer.'

'Oh, they'll do that all right,' I growled with certainty. 'There's a good thickness of rubberized canvas to give 'em protection from that missile-launcher out there.'

'Now you're bein' pessimistic, mister. He won't use no missile on a few tatty sailormen like them.'

'No?' I challenged, with a flicker of hope.

'No . . . 'e'll use his quick-firer forr'ad. Then small arms to finish off them what's still yellin'.'

The hope died abruptly. And so did the bow wave of the grey mini-warship. Once again she resumed her slow appraisal of the *Kamaran*'s concealed panic party.

'The plan's not going to work,' I groaned in frustration. 'Your idea of using your crew as bait isn't tempting enough, Trapp. He'll pick 'em off at long range . . .'

'Yes, it will, an' no, he won't!' Trapp retorted with a hint of asperity. 'I tell you Zarafiq's got to be sure I'm on the end o' his gunsights before he moves . . . I'm pretty special, you know. I'm the only one c'n really put him in queer street with 'is government pals, remember.'

I stared at him in outrage. Dammit, but he actually

looked pleased about it, conceited even. Personally I'd have thought that kind of distinction had all the desirability of being the only case of bubonic plague at a world health conference. But I wasn't Trapp.

'Then how's about you going over there an' giving yourself up so's the rest of us can go home,' I snarled, finally nettled by that self-assured smirk. 'And anyway – just say you are wrong? Say Zarafiq knows how we operated in the war, and doesn't risk coming any closer. Just opens fire from there regardless?'

'Then I'll apologize to the boys,' Trapp growled icily. 'An' save a lot o' money on end-o'-voyage bonuses.'

Which proved, if proof were still needed, that Edward Trapp had not changed one little bit . . .

. . . but then the sinister grey ship began to slide ahead again, much more determinedly than before. While Trapp ever so bleakly yanked back on the cocking handle of the tripod-mounted Soviet Kalashnikov PKS before him, then checked the link-belt ammunition feed.

And I did what might have seemed a rather odd thing to a casual observer. I simply placed my hands flat against the outboard end of the *Kamaran*'s bridge wing, and tensed my muscles. And prepared to meet Mister Zarafiq face to face.

Two hundred metres . . . one seventy . . . If Trapp still cherished any lingering conviction that all Ayrabs wus sloppy, then his chagrin must have matched my trepidation. They sensed that something was wrong, those Gahmanian Navy officers. The abandonment of the *Kamaran* had been too premature; too unexpected. I could see the white caps bent in anxious consultation with the frail, incongruous figure of the man who'd generated this still-senseless riddle; and while the tactical discussion went on, so the patrol-craft ratings remained closed up to their weapons with undeviating concentration. Something had to happen, and soon.

One sixty . . . one fifty-five . . . one fifty metres but slowing, swinging slightly as the cox'n spun the wheel. Still hesitant, and still as grimly alert.

'Come on,' Trapp growled, betraying his inner tension for the first time. 'Come on, c'mon, c'mon!'

Dejectedly I stole a hurried glance aft along the boat deck to where the second wave of our attack was assembled – and discovered my pessimism fully justified. Twenty per cent of our reserve wasn't there at all, yet – that was Mister Spew – while the trio of stranded Greeks were still trying desperately to blend in with the white-painted deckhousing, and Gorbals Wullie was managing to give a most successful impression of an irresolute ferret clutching a machinegun. Certainly there were five more loaded Czech machine-pistols from number two hold at instant readiness beside him, but it occurred to me they were more for self-protection rather than aggression.

'Told yer,' Trapp grunted abruptly. 'Di'n't I tell you they woul'n't use them missiles?'

I began to hope a little again. The warship was still closing slowly but now they'd secured from the launcher aft . . . only the three Arab ratings didn't just stand down; they immediately seized sub-machineguns and doubled smartly forward to line the near rail.

I think that was the moment when I finally did accept the reality of what Zarafiq was; and that there really were no empty cells awaiting the *Kamaran*'s crew back in Gahman. I think the crew got that impression too, and at much the same time; the unhappy mutters from the rafts below suddenly peaked on a crescendo of terror.

'DO something f'r God's sake,' I snarled, ashen-faced. 'Open fire if you're goin' to, Trapp. Before Zarafiq does.'

'Belay the advice, mister!' he snapped back tautly. 'We only got one chance . . . an' I ain't goin' to take it 'til we sees the whites o' their eyes.'

But his hand was clawlike on the butt of the Kalashnikov, and his finger was trembling against the trigger . . .

The loud-hailer, when it crackled, was almost as startling as a burst of gunfire. And Zarafiq's impeccable diction as enticing as honey.

'Captain Trapp. Please, my dear friend, desist from this rather odd and quite unnecessary behaviour.'

One twenty metres now, and circling to come from astern; just too far aft to vector the gun from where we lay . . .

'Show yourself, Captain. No need for such reticence. My naval associates beside me are most sympathetic to our mutual arrangement.'

The foredeck quick-firer swivelling all the time, though. And not on the rafts, dammit! A much higher elevation, allowing it to train along the line of the *Kamaran*'s main-deck bulwarks.

'They still suspect the ship,' I muttered sickly. 'Zarafiq is aware of how we operated before . . . he intends to take out the rafts and us at the same bloody time, Trapp.'

'The rafts, maybe. But not us yet, mister. Not unless they elevate that weapon a good few degrees,' Trapp calculated dispassionately. 'They're expectin' us somewhere along the centrecastle deck – we still got the drop on 'em from up 'ere . . .'

Ninety metres only, now, and one factor at least in our favour – she was nearing at as slow a speed as any gunner could have prayed for. Coming closer and closer, an unbelievable sitting duck, with the tension aboard her almost as evident as among our own gibbering bait in the rafts – or up here, on the *Kamaran*'s top decks, come to that.

'Might I suggest a ten-thousand-dollar bonus, Captain? What incentive that must be to common sense and . . .'

'Ten grand . . .' Trapp breathed ecstatically. Tearing my eyes away from the interceptor I stared at him uneasily; for the first time a hint of irresolution was evident. Money, to Trapp, was like an arrow in the heel for Achilles.

'Trapp. No, Trapp . . .' I cautioned appealingly.

Just as the growl of turbo-charged engines rose to a new note; to a surge of abruptly unleashed power . . . there was something wrong.

I swung hastily to face astern – and blinked. The water

under the patrol craft's counter had suddenly begun to swirl and froth, the bows rising as the flare below her stem surged higher and higher . . .

'They've fooled us, Trapp! They're making a speed run; goin' past to run down the rafts an' take us out at full power.'

'We still 'ave to wait . . .' he roared hopelessly. We both knew surprise was now the only card we had left.

Until . . .

'Awwww Jeeeeze!' Gorbals Wullie shrieked from the boat deck – and immediately began to fire in a panic-stricken reflex which, with a sub-machinegun at that range, could only act as a heaven-sent early warning to the attackers.

'Damn!' Trapp said.

'Trappppp!' I howled beseechingly.

'Well, go on then!' he bellowed back.

I shoved desperately – and the whole pre-loosened section at the extreme end of the bridge wing collapsed outboard, tumbling down to the sea below. At the time it had promised to be a most inadequate modification to make a battleship out of us; now it seemed utterly futile.

Trapp still snatched at the trigger of the heavy Kalashnikov, though. With a terrible, hopeless rage . . .

Gorbals Wullie may have compromised our deception through his agitated lack of self-control, but he probably saved the lives of a great many men in the rafts at the same time.

The warship was already turning in anticipation, sheering violently away as Trapp was forced to fire his first too-hasty burst. A line of high-velocity water-spouts exploded precisely between the accelerating patrol boat and our own hysterical panic party – only the FPB wasn't there any more. Already they were roaring at a tangent from our own heading with the yellow and blue ensign board flat in the wind and the cox'n bent low over his wheel.

Fifty metres . . . forty . . . still getting closer though as she overtook us. 'I'll kill 'im . . .' Trapp raged from suffused lips. 'I'll bloody *kill* that scrawny little bastaaaard!'

But I didn't know whether he meant Zarafiq or Gorbals Wullie. I didn't care all that much either – because that was the moment when the Kalashnikov jammed.

Simultaneously the quick-firer opened up with a measured rhythm. *Slam – slam – slam* . . . But they were having their troubles too. The gunlayer, locked against his restraining harness by the momentum of their un-anticipated turn, was still fighting for stability. Only he was winning . . . a diagonal slash of detonations suddenly climbed the *Kamaran*'s hull, peppered the after end of the centrecastle, converted the boat deck around Gorbals Wullie's carefully selected funk hole to a screeching, whining haze of splintered rails and leaping deck planks and colandered ventilators . . . maybe even bits of Gorbals Wullie.

It didn't matter. It couldn't matter. Not right then . . .

'Gerritfree . . .' I screamed. 'Gethatblockage*free*eeeee . . .'

Suddenly a small object sailed outwards, apparently from under the bridge deck where we crouched. A rock? A stone? Who the hell was throwing stones?

More explosions from the line of the davits now, coming even closer, f'r God's sake. And faces staring up from the racing craft now drawing abeam of us; white figures clinging against the centrifugal pull but with one more – Zarafiq – performing a funny, disoriented dance as he lost balance and staggered aft on the pocket-book fighting bridge.

The Kalashnikov, though. Why the hell was Trapp's Kalashnikov jammed now? Right when we needed it the mo . . . CHRIST!

Sub-machineguns yammering up at us as well, suddenly. Bullets seemingly flying everywhere. The windows in the after end of the *Kamaran*'s chartroom blowing inwards with a crash of diamond-bright splinters; a line of holes ripping through the woodwork a hand's breadth away from and parallel with my right leg . . . yet still more ridiculous things going on around us – another useless object arc-ing outboard to land with an insignificant plop under the slamming bow of the FPB . . .

'GetyerFOOToff . . .' Trapp stormed abruptly, volcanically. 'GetyerbloodyfootoffthebloodyAMMOBELT . . .'

I squirmed away in horror, releasing the jammed feed, and the Kalashnikov began to judder again – but too late. She was abeam of us now on a thunder of full power; ten seconds more and she'd be past and clear, and ready to return out of range and pick us off at leisure . . .

But she wouldn't need to come back. The quick-firer rounds were suddenly slamming into the top of the wheelhouse, chopping radar scanner and radio aerials, monkey island and standard compass into a smash of wreckage. And aiming even lower, correcting all the time . . . the after end of the bridge itself collapsing on top of us; Trapp bellowing obscenities and protecting himself while trying hopelessly to depress the muzzle of the gun at the same time . . .

I found myself blasted bodily sideways with my addled head poised over a hole which hadn't been there in the deck a moment ago. And Second Officer Dan'l Spew looked up cheerily through that brand-new hole, and said, ''Allo, Mister Cooper! 'Ow's things with you, then?'

Before drawing back his creaky arm to throw the third grenade he'd taken from that grey-painted box he'd been so enamoured with. Which did seem a rather futile gesture on the face of it, as they didn't appear to be detonating anyway.

It was a madness, of course. An exclusively Trapp-created world of dementia. Because I lay there, and watched that killer ship drawing away through the hole in the deck, and realized it could well be the last sight I would ever see . . . yet I still managed to be correct, ever so polite, to Mister Spew.

'Mister Spew,' I called, with the blood trickling relentlessly down my forehead.

'Yus, Mister Cooper?' he acknowledged with wide-eyed attentiveness.

'Don't bother to throw that hand-grenade, Mister Spew,' I urged considerately.

'No, Mister Cooper?' he queried, a little mystified certainly but only too anxious to be helpful.

'No,' I answered in tightly measured tones. 'Not . . . unless . . . you . . . pull . . . the . . . fucking . . . pin out first!'

It was a magnificent throw. It left Mister Spew's grasp as if projected by a strangely articulated ballista, and descended on its target with the accuracy of a Cruise Missile.

It exploded just as it reached the patrol craft's bridge and blew both the Arab captain and his first lieutenant into a ghastly, bloodied fusion. It stripped a large part of the cox'n's spine away and folded him over the wheel, locking it inextricably in the full-starboard-rudder mode. It blasted Mister Zarafiq – already teetering and off balance at the head of the ladder – in a very alive but shrieking and tweed-coat-flailing arc clean across the heads of her remaining crewmen, and finally deposited him in the boil of her wake.

She didn't stop to pick him up. Because there wasn't anyone left up there to stop her.

Still under full power she continued to describe a buffeting, flaring orbit away from the *Kamaran* as Trapp and I dragged ourselves erect and stared dumbly after her. Meanwhile Mister Spew stuck his head up through the cavity in the deck, and fixed us with an anthropoid and querying gaze.

'I suppose,' Mister Spew uttered, fatalistically but with the nearest hint he could ever get to of aggressiveness, 'I suppose I'm goin' ter get into trouble again, am I?'

Trapp found his voice eventually, and characteristically. 'Them grenades you wasted with not pullin' the pin. You realize 'ow much they're worth apiece, mister? How much them commies shoreside is goin' to dock off 've me fee?'

But there was no real bite to it, merely a shadow of his usual nit-picking disparagement. And then, just as I turned with fatalistic apprehension to search for the corpse of the late Gorbals Wullie in the shambles of the strafed boat deck, Trapp added wildly, 'Ohhhhh, hell!'

And I swung back disconcerted to catch sight of him galloping for the engine telegraph, still rearing crookedly above the debris of the wheelhouse.

I frowned, took one look out to sea where the Gahmanian craft had taken off on her crazy, uncontrolled departure – and then I too was running. This time for the bridge wing overlooking the rafts.

I didn't even hesitate when I saw the tiny figure splashing dementedly at the spot where Mister Zarafiq had performed his grenade-assisted dive. I just flung myself full length, stuck my head out over the end of the bridge, and waved frantically to the pallid, pleading faces gazing up at me.

'Padle!' I roared. 'She's comin' back – so jus' shut up. An' paddle . . .'

Even then we might have avoided her if Trapp hadn't put the engine ahead like that. But he did, and we didn't, which was typical of the whole bloody voyage anyway.

By the time the rogue warship had come round on a reciprocal course to head straight for us she must have been doing forty knots; probably with an unwitting Arab engineer rating, blind and still below in her engineroom, trying to make her go even faster in what he would have assumed was a tactical withdrawal, not a suicidal return to the fray.

The floundering howls of Sheik Rabah Moinzadeh alias Zarafiq were once again submerged in the wake of the homing runaway as she slammed past him for a second time on her five-thousand-horsepower circuit. Her forward gun was deserted now, its crew racing hopelessly aft and away from where the *Kamaran* must now be rising before them like a high-speed steell cliff. Only one seaman still had the presence of mind to clamber through the wreckage of her bridge to wrestle vainly with her locked wheel and throttles.

She was still swinging, though. Still veering to pass close under – but possibly clear – of our looming bows . . .

I had the ridiculous impression that the life-rafts were also doing forty knots on a blur of paddles – the other way! But that was only because I was still dazed, and the *Kamaran* had begun to slide through the water too, leaving them behind.

I saw what was going to happen. I was even shouting, 'Astern, Trapp! Come astern, man . . .' when the warship finally hit.

She only caught our stem a glancing blow, but it was enough to capsize her instantly. Her after end slammed round in a spraying, crazy arc under the momentum of her swing, and she continued to skip and roll appallingly across an ejected carpet of smashed and dying crewmen . . . while the *Kamaran* herself veered to port – almost chasing the cavorting, disintegrating hulk – but then I sensed, rather than saw, the contraction in the water ahead, and the white flash which seemed to freeze the very sea itself . . . and I was scrabbling for what little cover remained behind the bridge front when submerging electronics short-circuited and the Gahmanian missiles started to explode.

They seemed to last for a long time, those underwater detonations, with the *Kamaran* wincing and bucking in pain as blow after submarine blow struck her deep under her belly. For our party floating astern in the rafts it must have presented a nightmare of concussion, transmitted up through the thin floors of the fragile craft, while for Mister Zarafiq – totally unprotected from the pressures below the surface – it could only have offered a torment to satisfy even the vengeful ambition of Trapp.

Finally it was over.

Stiffly I uncurled yet again, uncovered my head, and looked cautiously around – and then gaped; conscious of an embarrassment I'd never have believed possible.

For Trapp was crying. A suddenly old and very tired man. Just crying . . .

He was simply standing there, gazing aft to where Gorbals Wullie had been before the action began, only now there were only twisted rails and the black pocks of violence, and three shaken Greek seamen trying to extricate themselves from the mess. A Thompson sub-machinegun lay there too, right on the edge of a torn crater where the deck slipped away to the sea, but there was no one left beside it.

Pulling myself to my feet I wiped the blood from my eyes and staggered over to Trapp, but he didn't seem even to be aware of me, didn't make any attempt to conceal the grief which shook his bowed shoulders. Tentatively I put out a hand and touched him gently, helplessly, as Mister Spew joined us from below.

'Like losin' a pet dog,' Mister Spew intoned sonorously. ''E wus just like a dog, wus Wullie. A little Pekingese puppy wiv a flat face. An' a big mouth . . .'

'A Scottie dog,' Trapp snuffled. ''E wus a Scottie dog what I loved like . . . like . . .'

'Er . . . like a dog?' suggested Mister Spew somewhat confusingly.

'But ah'm no' a dog – ah'm more like a tiger!' the voice of Gorbals Wullie interjected wii h a curiously unspiritual excitement. 'Here, did yous no' see me throw they Arabs intae total confusion, did ye? Man, but wis I no' a real snapshot wi' the Tommy gun, wis ah?'

We turned slowly, speechlessly. The apparition before us looked far too insanitary and solid for a ghost.

'Where the 'ell did you come from?' the bereaved pet fancier finally demanded with a somewhat less than joyous expression of welcome.

'The port side,' offered the reincarnated and suddenly uncertain Fido. 'But ah'm tryin' tae tell you how ah scunnered they navy lads . . .'

'An' what – ' further demanded Trapp in a tone which caused even Mister Spew to move discreetly out of range – 'wus you doing on the port side, when they wus attackin' us from the starboard side?'

'I wis . . . er . . . well, me bein' third officer, Captin, I wis doin' my duty an' . . . well . . . makin' sure no cowardly sailors wis hidin' round there . . .'

Trapp kicked him all the way to the bottom of the ladder. And then glared down, and took a deep breath, and bawled volcanically, 'Third officer? I seen better third officers what coul'n't tie a granny knot! I seen third officers what had been drownded in a flooded compartment f'r a week, an' still wi' more brains than you. Third officer, you says? I seen camel drivers in the middle o' the Kalahari Desert what 'as more idea o' seamanship than you, stupid! So it's an ordinary seaman you are again from now on, yer sneaky Scotch egg. An ordin'ry seaman – an' about the ordinariest bloody seaman I ever did set eyes on, at that . . .'

I tiptoed discreetly into the wheelhouse and began to turn the *Kamaran* on a reciprocal which would take us back to the rafts, and whatever was left of Mister Zarafiq.

I didn't think I'd ever seen Trapp so happy; so blissfully happy and relieved . . .

CHAPTER FOURTEEN

Most of the panic party had to be assisted up the ladder from the rafts. Some, through shock and fright, had to be manhandled up the ship's side on the end of a safety line. Others weren't even in a condition to do that . . .

Mister Zarafiq, for instance, was all smashed up inside; the force of those submarine explosions must have split his intestines like a rabbit's under a hammer. Yet he was still alive, still semiconscious when I brought him to the *Kamaran* and slipped a bowline under his limp arms for them to haul him to the deck.

I followed up the pilot ladder, rung by painful rung, with the inert form of the moaning Arab rising jerkily beside me. Oh, I tried to cushion him as much as I could but Trapp wasn't very gentle, and Mister Zarafiq learned, perhaps for the first time, just what it was like to be on the receiving end of someone else's callousness.

Yet even when we'd nearly reached the top the Arab's torment wasn't over. For Trapp simply stopped hauling, secured the line, leaned out over the bulwark – and smiled.

It would have been better – more hopeful for Zarafiq – if his rescuer had struck him.

''Allo, Mister Z,' Trapp said, ever so friendly. 'Feelin' a bit crook, are yer?'

Zarafiq merely dangled there, dripping water from his expensive tweed coat and black blood from his slack mouth, and whimpering softly.

'For God's sake, Trapp,' I called urgently.

But Trapp just continued to smile as if he hadn't heard me. Or didn't intend to.

'You'll appreciate, what wi' you being a business man too, that when an extra service is called for on a contract, then there's gotter be an extra charge to cover it – agreed,

Mister Z? Oh, I do hope you don't mind me callin' you Mister Zarafiq, Sheik. Seein' it was your idea in the first place?'

'Trapp!' I appealed again, staring anxiously up at the group of faces now watching sullenly from the rail. But apart from Gorbals Wullie and Mister Spew, heaving grimly on a second recovery line further along, nobody moved; nobody raised a hint of protest.

'So as there never was no clause agreed which gave you yourself a berth aboard the *Kamaran*,' Trapp continued remorselessly, 'then I'm quite within me contractual rights to ask a little more before I do. Let's say four questions, Mister Z . . . four easy-to-answer little questions, eh?'

'Please, Captain . . .' Zarafiq whispered.

Trapp just kept right on smiling.

'The first is simple . . . like where's the rest o' me money? The balance outstanding on completion of contract?'

'Trapp!'

Zarafiq's lips moved imperceptibly. 'On shore. The group who are expecting the cargo. I could not tell them it would be . . . unnecessary?'

'Unnecessary, Mister Zarafiq? Are you suggestin' this cargo wasn't meant to reach Gahman, then? Which brings me to me second question – why did you go to so much trouble to hire me as master of this ship? What's the special quality I 'ave that made me so attractive, mister?'

Zarafiq's eyes opened and he gazed pleadingly up at Trapp. 'Please, for pity's sake, Captain. No more questions until . . .'

Trapp looked terribly disappointed. He brought his hand up from behind the bulwark and there was a knife in it. He laid the knife regretfully on the rope securing Mister Zarafiq . . .

'You are a dishonest man . . .' Zarafiq screamed in terror, 'but with one reliable attribute – you can be depended upon to cheat your employer . . .'

I could hear the sharp intake of breath along the rail. The ship rolled uneasily, fretfully, and we swung away from the hull, suspended over thirty feet of nothing. Zarafiq moaned like an animal in pain as we slammed back into the steel side.

'It don't quite answer the question,' Trapp said, not at all offended or anything. 'I asked you why you needed me; a bloke you seemed certain would swindle you out o' this very valuable cargo?'

'Let him up, Trapp,' I snarled, my own arms beginning to ache with the strain of clinging to the ladder. 'Let him up, you sadistic bastard.'

'I'll let 'im down inna minnit,' Trapp promised coldly. 'If 'e don't answer *jaldi*.'

'I was in a most embarrassing position,' Zarafiq sobbed. 'While I am a minister in a pro-Western administration I have also become . . . politically affiliated to the communist cause.'

'You mean you been takin' money from the Reds as well,' Trapp translated. It was a language he understood intimately. 'Go on, mister – where does the *Kamaran* figure in this?'

'My . . . my Marxist associates let it be known they were prepared to offer a great deal of money to anyone who could provide adequate arms to ensure a successful *coup d'état* in Gahman. I was foolish enough to suggest that I, and certain Egyptian colleagues, would be able to fulfil such a need . . .'

Zarafiq swung away from the side again and spun helplessly, a great and wicked spider enmeshed in his own web, which fed on corruption and grew bloated on the corpses of people who died in wars of his making. This time when I caught the appeal in his agonized eyes I stayed silent; I even turned away in contempt.

'Go on,' Trapp encouraged, toying almost absently with the knife.

'But . . . but there were penalties. I realized that, having accepted payment from the Communist Liberation Front, I would have to be seen making the most strenuous efforts to ensure that the *Kamaran*'s cargo avoided . . . ah . . . interception. By those anxious to prevent its delivery; fools such as Chang, motivated only by greed . . .'

'Tut, tut!' commiserated Trapp, shocked to his very core by the perfidy of persons less honourable than he and Mister Zarafiq. 'An' then there's the capitalists, ain't there? Like the Yanks an' the British – only interested in stoppin' blokes like you from makin' a few bob because that could upset their friendly strategic bases around the Med . . . only there's one thing puzzles me a bit about that, Mister Z . . .'

I saw him looking pointedly at me with a challenging grin on his lips as he continued, '. . . f'r a time Mister Cooper here 'ad the distinct impression the British wanted the arms to get through. Or they did originally. Now why ever should a true-blue country like the Brits be anxious to see a pro-Western crowd like the Gahmanians outa favour?'

I turned to listen again. I already knew, but I still needed to hear it again, just so's I could believe my admiral for once.

'Oil prices,' the racked man gasped. 'My government had adopted a policy forced upon them by the Americans – of holding them down; of stabilization. But politics can create strange bedfellows . . . North Sea oil has now made the United Kingdom one of the world's largest producers – and any potential exporter would be most anxious to see hawks, even communist-controlled hawks such as Libya, compelling OPEC to raise the price of crude . . . please, I beg of you, Captain!'

'Then why did the British change their mind, Zarafiq?' Trapp continued to press as though Zarafiq hadn't even been hurt. 'Why do they suddenly want ter stop this cargo just as much as the Yanks?'

'Because we – my government – have also changed our minds. We have now agreed to raise the price of oil, meaning there is no longer any advantage to the British in aiding a Marxist take-over in Gahman.'

'Very interestin' – but you haven't explained the need f'r my services even now,' Trapp growled doggedly, toying with the knife a little more ostentatiously than before. 'Go on, Mister Z. We're all listenin' avidly.'

'I am a government minister – and a very rich one. I have no illusions regarding what would happen to me should the proletariat topple my party, Captain. Justice would have to be seen to be done, even to those who assisted discreetly . . . just as it was essential for me to be seen to employ a top-class captain by my communist friends.'

'Ahhhh,' breathed Trapp with enormous satisfaction. 'Because they woul'n't realize you'd made bloody certain I *would* divert the cargo by makin' me a bit disenchanted from the start. You're a very sneaky Ayrab, Mister Zarafiq . . .'

'Let him up, now,' I snarled, sickened by the barbarity of it all. But Trapp shook his head; still looked as implacable as ever.

'Four questions, I said, mister. He's got two correct so far. Zarafiq. Do yer hear me, Zarafiq?'

The dangling man seemed smaller now, shrivelled in his private torment. 'Pleeeease, Captain! We made a bargain . . .?'

'And I won't cheat yer, Mister Z. Not this time I won't. Two more questions f'r you to answer like I said – but you got to answer them in full, mind. You got to get a hundred per cent f'r each one.'

'Hurry! Please hurry.'

'Number three,' Trapp announced levelly, only the smile had gone suddenly. 'Them three Pakistanis on the old *Last Hope* . . . did you order Fadel ter cut their throats, Zarafiq? Did you 'ave them gutted deliberately, mister?'

A wave larger than the rest struck the side of the *Kamaran*. Zarafiq pendulumed away again, and back with an excruciating scream. He shook his head pleadingly, as if disbelieving such previously unimagined horrors.

'Did you?'

'Yes! Yesssss! They were nothing. I knew – I intended their deaths to anger you; to ensure you would deceive me . . .'

The look in Trapp's eyes was terrible to see. I watched the knife hypnotically – everyone watched that knife and the way it trembled in Trapp's grasp. Even Gorbals Wullie and Dan'l Spew had turned by now, leaving their own burden suspended, just like Mister Zarafiq, high above the waiting sea.

Yet when Trapp spoke again his voice was still very quiet.

'Last question, Zarafiq. All you got to do is give me the solution to one small problem. It's a difficulty you've sort o' created yourself anyway – so it shoul'n't be too hard to answer, should it now?'

'Hurry . . .' the agony that was Zarafiq choked. 'For mercy's sake, what is it you wish me to tell you?'

Trapp simply pointed along the hull a short distance; towards the recovery line still grasped by Wullie and Spew.

A . . . a Thing swayed gently on the end of it. A pathetic, ghastly Thing which twirled and bobbed and still dripped a steady stream of engine oil and seawater to the empty life-raft below.

There was a charred hole drilled right through the face of it; a hole roughly the diameter of a quick-firer round from, say, a Gahman Navy patrol boat. But it was still just possible to recognize that the Thing wasn't simply a Thing after all – that it was actually the pitiful, incredibly forlorn corpse of Maabud whatsit, lately chief engineer of the *Kamaran*.

'You can come aboard, Zarafiq,' Trapp said with incontestable sincerity, 'just as soon as you've explained to me how to make that harmless little man run about on deck again. An' feel the wind on 'is face. An' laugh an' be happy, or cry an' be frightened . . .'

Mister Zarafiq was screaming even before Trapp cut the rope. He continued to shriek all the way down to the sea, after I'd lunged for him, but missed.

But ethics were ethics, even in the game of treachery chosen by Zarafiq himself. And in defence of Trapp – he really had kept to his part of the contract.

Mister Zarafiq had actually been the one who'd failed to fulfil the conditions of the penalty clause . . .

CHAPTER FIFTEEN

The shore was less than twelve miles off by the time I'd recovered from my nausea and climbed heavily to the shattered bridge. I wouldn't even have gone up then – but I still had a job to do.

I knew it was hopeless the moment he turned and saw me standing there.

'No,' Trapp growled emphatically. 'I ain't goin' to sink her, mister. Not f'r you, not f'r nobody! There's still a lot o' contract payment outstandin' and I'm planning to deliver – and collect.'

'Dammit but you're still British,' I exploded savagely. 'This is the Mediterranean, Trapp, and God knows the Soviets have a big enough hold in North Africa already. You deliver those arms and they'll have a damn sight tighter one.'

'Yeah? Then how come even you wus originally so keen to see the arms delivered, when I wasn't? Well I'll tell yer, Miller – because it all comes down to money in the end. Even the British Governmint wus prepared to see the Reds in power when there was a chance it'd shove the price of oil up an' up . . . an' anyway, I ain't been proper British f'r a long time. I ain't even been back there f'r years – apart from on the Blackbird run, at least.'

I swallowed. I wished he hadn't said that, especially not in view of the conversation I'd had a few minutes ago with a certain British admiral. I made one last, rather self-conscious attempt to wave the Union Flag.

'So I can't even appeal to your patriotism. You've actually sunk that low, Trapp?'

He made an unnecessarily coarse gesture which tended to confirm the word he used at the same time. I took a deep breath and played my last card.

'Then I'm . . . ordering you to scuttle this ship, Trapp. Or at least turn her round and hand her over to a Western power.'

He stared at me. I stared back at him. It was like watching a pressure cooker with a jammed safety valve.

And then he blew off. Gently at first; ominously gently as the heat built up.

'Orderin' me, mister? Did you say you wus . . . ordering me?'

I sneaked an appealing glance towards the wrecked wheelhouse. Gorbals Wullie and Mister Spew stood listening – yes, even Spew was receiving Trapp loud and clear this time – and the only previous occasion I'd ever seen two individuals preparing for such instantaneous flight was when that bloody scuttling charge had been liable to go off in the engineroom.

The one I wished so desperately could go off now. Immediately.

'*Orderin' me, mister . . . ?*'

'By the authority vested in me under Queen's Regulations and the Naval Discipline Act,' I heard myself mutter – then I thought *Oh, the HELL with it!* and finished off recklessly, 'I've got a radio transmitter on board, Trapp. I've been using it to talk to an admiral – an' he says you'll bloody well do what you're told because . . . er . . . because . . .'

I ran out of courage then. It had never happened to me before in an argument with Trapp; but I'd never had to tell him anything like I was supposed to tell him now, either. I hadn't seen quite that look on his face before, come to that. Or not since the moment when he'd cut Mister Zarafiq's umbilical cord, anyway . . .

'Because? Because what?'

'Because you're . . . still an officer in the Royal Navy,' I choked weakly. 'Because after the war you never turned up to demobilize, Trapp. You've always been posted as "Missing, believed killed". And that means you've never actually been . . . well . . . written off the books, so to speak.

An' that means you're still a full Commander, RN. And that means you gotter carry out orders or they'll bloody well hang you!'

'Awwwww Jeeeeze . . .' whispered a pop-eyed Gorbals Wullie, in the most apprehensive croak I'd ever heard. 'They gone an' done it tae him again. *F'r the second time . . .*'

He didn't say anything at all. Not at first.

He simply stamped off the bridge, demolished my cabin piece by piece until he found the radio in the wardrobe, had a few words of confirmation with a presumably equally-apoplectic Admiral Charlie Tango Control . . . and then gave the Royal Navy his answer.

It wasn't too difficult to hazard a guess at what his answer had been – there were still bits of radio valves and things embedded in the toe of his boot when he returned to the *Kamaran*'s bridge.

I watched him anxiously; worried in case he would be successful in avoiding a heart attack. I now had less than an hour in which to sink the *Kamaran*, and very little prospect otherwise of doing so.

And then, suddenly, I had no prospects at all.

'Mister Spew.'

Very ordinary seaman Gorbals Wullie let out a pent-up shriek of tension and tried to hide behind the wheel. Mister Spew bumbled uncertainly over and gave Trapp a one-eyed stare of ferocious determination.

'Yus, Captin?'

Trapp indicated me with an icy jerk of his chin. 'Ask this officer where he's hid me detonators, Mister Spew. The detonators f'r me scuttlin' charges.'

'Why . . . er . . . why don't yer ask 'im yerself, Captin?' Mister Spew frowned.

'Because I ain't speakin' to 'im. That's why.'

'The captin wants ter know where's the detonators f'r the captin's scuttlin' charges, Mister Cooper.' Mister Spew asked lugubriously.

'Get stuffed,' I muttered morosely. 'Mister Spew.'

'Smash 'is fuckin' 'ead in,' Trapp commanded, staring pointedly into the middle distance.

I watched Mister Spew's one good arm rise obligingly, if a little unwillingly. It looked rather like a steam hammer operated by King Kong's big brother.

'. . . under the emergency wheel in the tiller flat,' I snarled urgently.

'Go and get 'em, Mister Spew,' Trapp said with deep satisfaction. Or was it disappointment?

Then he condescended to fix me with a crafty, only-too-familiar leer of triumph. 'Oh, an' Mister Spew?'

Spew hesitated at the head of the ladder. 'Yus, Captin?'

'We knows what ter do with them detonators, don't we, Mister Spew? We knows precisely what to do wi' them detonators, don't we?'

'Ho yus, Captin,' affirmed Mister Spew as he shuffled below, leaving an unsettlingly Cyclopean and conspiratorial wink hanging above the ladder. 'We knows all about what ter do wiv them detonators.'

'You bastard,' I spat after he'd gone. 'They're your last chance to stay decent, Trapp. Once Spew ditches them you've really joined the outcasts – the international league of sewer rats.'

'I ain't speakin' to you, mister,' Trapp said complacently. 'But if I wus – then I'd say it's still better than joinin' the Royal Navy. Especially f'r the third time . . .'

I opened my mouth to retort, then closed it again with a snap. For a long moment I couldn't take my eyes away from a point just over his shoulder; a point where the water met the sky in a misty, seaward forming of the horizon.

And then I began to grin. For the first time this voyage it really was my turn to grin.

Trapp glowered at me suspiciously.

'What're you grinnin' for?' he demanded, changeably ill-tempered again. 'I won't 'ave my chief officers grinnin' like Cheshire cats when they're on the bridge, d'ye hear?'

'You can't ask me that,' I reminded him recklessly. 'You aren't even speaking to me, so how can you ask me anyth . . .'

'I'll speak when I wants, how I wants, an' ter who I wants, mister!' Trapp roared. Only there wasn't any real fire to it; just a trace of uncertainty.

'And I'm not your chief officer any more either,' I persisted spitefully. 'As far as I know I'm not your anything any more, Trapp. But if I was – then I'd be your First Lieutenant . . . Commander.'

'Don't say that. Don't bloody call me that . . . I already told both you an' your admiral – I ain't in no Royal Navy no longer an' that's final.'

'Final?'

'Final!'

'But what about the Naval Discipline Act?'

'F**** and **** and **** the Naval bloody Discipline Act!'

I took one further, intensely satisfying glance over his shoulder and sighed.

'Well, I suppose you'd better repeat that to them, sir. Seein' they've sent a *Leander* class frigate all this way, just to enforce it.'

Of course I shouldn't have been so complacent. I should have known Trapp better than to assume he intended to be diverted from his long-awaited pot of gold by anything so irrelevant as a fighting friate of the Royal Navy.

Even as he saw it, while the disbelief was still turning to sour resentment, he was on his way through to the skeletal wreckage of the chartroom and grabbing for the dividers.

Suddenly uneasy, I waited in the wheelhouse beside a white-faced and trembling – in other words normal – Gorbals Wullie, who could only mutter over and over again, 'Jeeeeze, och Jeeze butta friggit . . . Aw Jeeze a friggit, Captin . . .'

'Shut up an' steer f'r the coast,' Trapp bellowed back

without lifting his head. 'An' ring down f'r all the speed we got, stupid!'

'You can't do it, Trapp!' I shouted. 'She can sink us with one salvo from her weapons systems. Give in, man. Pretend you meant to conform with their orders all the time. I swear I'll back you up . . .'

The revolutions under the deck began to build until every loose item in the *Kamaran*'s wheelhouse – and there were plenty of 'em by then – was chattering and shuddering and racketing frenetically. Then Trapp rushed out of the chartroom with a sneer of triumph and waved the tattered chart aggressively.

'See? There's less than a forty-minnit run to the shore, *mister*! And once I takes her inside them shoals there ain't nobody, not even your fancy grey-funnel line, c'n touch me . . . because they ain't going to overhaul the *Kamaran* in forty minutes, are they? From that distance off they'd need ter be an aeryoplane, they would. An' a frigate sure ain't no aeryoplane.'

I shuffled nervously, all my previous glee shattered by the anxiety of what might happen. Either way I was bound to be the loser.

'But they can still fire at us, Trapp. Guns . . . missiles . . . we haven't a chance.'

The contempt on his face was only matched by the derision. 'Fire at us? They won't fire at us, mister. They won't fire on a vessel flyin' the flag o' a foreign power – and in someone else's territorial waters, laddie? 'Ave you forgot that's the Royal Navy out there, then? The fair-play, lose-wi'-a-stiff-upper-lip gentleman's navy, mister . . .'

There was a distant flash from the horizon, and then a scream like a giant ripping a canvas hatch-cover clean across. Trapp's mouth stayed open for as long as it took for me and Gorbals Wullie to hit the deck.

The shell, when it exploded, lifted half a ton of Mediterranean Sea above the bridge, then dropped it all inboard as a torrent of cordite-tainted spray. The remaining sections of the wheelhouse deckhead collapsed around Trapp to the accompaniment of not entirely unfamiliar howls of terror from the after accommodation.

Nobody moved as Mister Spew crawled the last few steps of the ladder on his hands and knees and stared round blankly, trying hard to think. Then his face cleared as he remembered why he'd come, and he scowled earnestly up at Trapp.

'I come ter tell you, Captin. I don't suppose no one else 'as noticed yet, but there's a *warship* over there on the port quarter . . .'

'Let me guess the bloody rest . . .' Trapp screamed back in fury. 'Like now you're gonna tell me she could fire at us any soddin' minnit.'

'Bless me if you isn't pure magic, Captin,' Mister Spew said, the star of worship bright in his solitary eye. ''Owever can you guess at the thoughts what's still in me 'ead . . .?'

Of course she never did catch us – the frigate. As soon as Trapp called their bluff, kept right on running inshore despite that warning shot, the grey and impossibly distant *Leander* hauled off to starboard and simply watched in frustration while Trapp conned the *Kamaran* into the narrowing reaches of the late Mister Zarafiq's secret rendezvous.

He was cocky about it, too. No sooner had we entered than he ambled right out on the wing of the bridge and stuck two fingers in the air towards the White Ensign which had tried unavailingly to claim him – the most unlikely of all ulikely naval officers – for the third time in his misbegotten career.

Then he grinned at me. It was a sardonic, totally unrepentant grin but I couldn't hate him for it any more. Not now. Because I was seeing the old Trapp again; Trapp the Buccaneer, Trapp the Survivor, Trapp the everebullient. And suddenly I knew I loved him very much . . . on occasions.

He pointed ahead, up the river to where the communist

trucks were already waiting like patient crocodiles along the bank.

'It's inevitable, mister,' he called with irrepressible conceit. 'I makes a few dollars, loses a few dollars – but I don't ever, never lose the war . . .'

Which was a rather ironic claim to make, really.

Seeing that was the moment when the *Kamaran* started to blow up!

Her bows went first, chopped clean off by the force of the blast. Then a second explosion, deep inside her. And a third . . .

I felt Trapp cannon violently into me, followed by Second Officer Spew, and suddenly the whole bloody heap of us were displaced for a second time as a screeching Gorbals Wullie burrowed underneath the pile like a refuge-seeking mole in a cloth cap. I didn't have time to tell him it wasn't the best place to be – seeing the explosions were coming from below at the time.

'What the hell . . .?' spluttered Trapp as a fourth detonation followed.

And then a fifth . . . The *Kamaran* began to fall over sideways while water was already rushing and gurgling excitedly up the bridge. A gaily-coloured life-raft – one of the ones originally inflated on the deck as the panic party abandoned – came bobbing past and I grappled automatically for the painter.

'It's those charges,' I said faintly, disbelievingly. 'Your scuttling charges, Trapp. F'r some inexplicable reason every bloody one of them must have gone off together.'

Mister Spew clambered into the life-raft and sat there beaming at us, bouncing gently up and down in the displacing water. He did look pleased; positively delighted, in fact.

'This time,' he announced proudly, but with the slightest suspicion of appeal. 'Now this time you *gotter* admit I done everythin' proper, Captin. Five outa five. That's . . . er . . . near enough to about ninety per cent.'

Trapp stared at him. And I stared at him. Even Gorbals Wullie crawled tentatively out from under. And stared at him.

'What did you do right, Mister Spew?' I asked eventually. And for the very last time.

'Them detonators, Mister Cooper.' He smiled happily. 'I knew exac'ly what ter do wiv 'em, jus' like the captin said I would . . . Because I ain't so daft, really – I 'aven't never forgotten how upset 'e wus that last time. When them bombs didn't go off . . .'

The ebbing current drifted us steadily out to sea, the flagship of an aimless little flotilla of rubbish from the *Kamaran*. Most of her unhappy crew were riding the river with us, all clinging grimly to hope and odd bits of ship.

Trapp still hadn't said a word, simply slouched in the bottom of the orange raft in inconsolable gloom and staring astern at the hulk of the only decent vessel he'd ever commanded, now lying capsized and nearly submerged on the bed of that desolate creek.

Already the communist trucks had gone; stolen hurriedly away in search of another Mister Zarafiq; another revolution . . . but most emphatically not another Trapp.

He only spoke once in all the time it took us to cross over the bar and return to the Mediterranean in our ragamuffin convoy. It was a brief response to Gorbals Wullie – a truly Trapp-type flash of petulance – when the wizened little Scot looked back at what might have been, then offered loyally, 'Never mind, Captin. We still got half o' Mister Z's advance. We'll hae a braw time back at the Red Sweetwater wan o' these days, eh?'

'No *we* won't, stupid!' Trapp had snarled in momentary animation. 'You still ain't got nuthin', ordinary seaman! 'Cause your half wus in the second half . . . the half we di'n't get, see?'

'He's gettin' better,' Wullie announced joyfully. 'Did ah no' tell ye he'd get better, then?'

We drifted a little further in strained silence. I watched

the frigate coming towards us and felt happy – yet strangely sad, all at the same time. But I wasn't alone in my satisfaction; not when I glanced over and saw the look on Mister Spew's anthropoid but amiable features.

He smiled wistfully, proudly as his one good eye caught mine.

'Five out o' five, Mister Cooper,' he said. 'I ain't never got five out o' five for nothin'. Not ever before . . .'

Trapp only stirred at the last minute. When the frigate had lost way and her boats were already slipping from the falls to come and salvage us.

Suddenly he sat up and frowned. Before an all-too-familiar expression of inspired guile wiped the last traces of gloom from the ageless features.

'That business about me bein' a Royal Navy commander, mister. You sure it still holds good – that there ain't no one c'n change it?'

'The admiral told me so himself. They posthumously promoted you to full rank the last time you were killed,' I assured him. But I thought I was only cheering him up at the time; not being bloody stupid.

'An' that frigate there. What rank o' officer would be in complete charge, then?'

I shrugged. 'A lieutenant-commander, probably. Certainly no higher than a full commander like you. Why?'

'So that would make me the . . . ah . . . senior officer then. 'Cause I been a full commander since jus' after nineteen forty-two – an' there ain't hardly no one left in the Royal Navy that was innit in forty-two.'

An uneasy feeling gripped my stomach but I forced it to go away. No. No, not even Trapp could conceive of anything quite so . . . so Machiavellian as that. Could he?

'While that, in its turn, means the captain o' that frigate has ter obey all my orders, don't it? Or else I could 'ave 'im charged, couldn't I, mister . . . under the Naval Discipline Act, no less.'

I stared at him. Gorbals Wullie was staring at him, too, with a mixture of trepidation and suppressed delight. But

Trapp wasn't looking at us any more – now he only had eyes for that beautiful, shiny, expensive and lethal warship out there. Already they were proprietary eyes; cunning, oh so characteristically avaricious eyes . . .

'Trapp,' I begged. 'Please, Trapp, don't even think about it.'

But he was a long way away by then. A whole inventive and outrageously double-dealing world away.

'A commercial-minded bloke could do such a lot with a frigate,' he breathed dreamily; determinedly.

'No, Trapp! Pleeeeease . . .'

'Oh, what a lot 'e could do. What business opportunities 'e could take advantage of . . .' mused the indestructible Captain Edward Trapp, the very last of the ocean pirates.

'. . . with a whole frigate. An' guns. And even *missiles* of 'is very own . . .'

Antony Trew

His novels of action and danger, at sea and on
land, have been highly praised. A Royal Navy
Commander during World War II, Antony Trew
served in the Mediterranean and the Western
Approaches, and was awarded the D.S.C.

His books include:

THE SOUKOUR DEADLINE 70p
THE MOONRAKER MUTINY 70p
THE SEA BREAK 65p
KLEBER'S CONVOY 50p
THE ZHUKOV BRIEFING 70p

Fontana Books

Dudley Pope

'Takes over the helm from Hornblower . . . Dudley Pope knows all about the sea and can get the surge of it into his writing.' *Daily Mirror*

'An author who really knows the ropes of Nelson's navy.' *Observer*

'The best of the Hornblower successors.' *Sunday Times*

RAMAGE 85p
RAMAGE AND THE DRUM BEAT 80p
RAMAGE AND THE FREEBOOTERS 85p
RAMAGE AND THE GUILLOTINE 80p
RAMAGE'S DIAMOND 85p
RAMAGE'S MUTINY 85p
RAMAGE AND THE REBELS 85p

Fontana Paperbacks

Duncan Kyle

'The outstanding thriller-writer discovery of the seventies.'
Evening News

WHITEOUT! 75p
A CAGE OF ICE 80p
FLIGHT INTO FEAR 80p
TERROR'S CRADLE 80p

Fontana Paperbacks

Fontana Paperbacks

Fontana is a leading paperback publisher of fiction and non-fiction, with authors ranging from Alistair MacLean, Agatha Christie and Desmond Bagley to Solzhenitsyn and Pasternak, from Gerald Durrell and Joy Adamson to the famous Modern Masters series.

In addition to a wide-ranging collection of internationally popular writers of fiction, Fontana also has an outstanding reputation for history, natural history, military history, psychology, psychiatry, politics, economics, religion and the social sciences.

All Fontana books are available at your bookshop or newsagent; or can be ordered direct. Just fill in the form and list the titles you want.

FONTANA BOOKS, Cash Sales Department, G.P.O. Box 29, Douglas, Isle of Man, British Isles. Please send purchase price, plus 8p per book. Customers outside the U.K. send purchase price, plus 10p per book. Cheque, postal or money order. No currency.

NAME (Block letters)

ADDRESS